Quite an Undertaking:
Devon's Story

ALSO BY BARBARA L. CLANTON

THE GRASSE RIVER SERIES
Quite an Undertaking: Devon's Story (Book One)
Rebecca's Story (Book Two) ... <Coming Soon>

THE CLARKSONVILLE SERIES
Out of Left Field: Marlee's Story (Book One)
Tools of Ignorance: Lisa's Story (Book Two)
Going, Going, Gone: Susie's Story (Book Three)
Stealing Second: Sam's Story (Book Four)
Out at Home (Book Five)
Tools of the Devil (Book Six)
Going Under (Book Seven)
Stealing Hope (Book Eight)

THE WHICKETT SERIES
Art for Art's Sake: Meredith's Story (Book One)
More Than Roommates: Dani's Story (Book Two)

THE GIRLS' SPORTS SERIES (Children's Books Ages 9-12)
Bases Loaded
Side Out
Live, Love, Lacrosse

QUITE AN UNDERTAKING
Devon's Story

BOOK ONE IN THE GRASSE RIVER SERIES

BARBARA L. CLANTON

Paperback ISBN   978-1-953734-39-6

First Edition 2024
9 8 7 6 5 4 3 2 1

Cover design by Sarah (Forcoverservice)

Published by:
Bibi Books Publishing Company, LLC

Dedication

For my brothers, Paul and John. With you two strong guys on either end, it was easy being the middle child. Thanks for being so supportive when I confided in you about the "please shift" that life dealt me. Your support way back then helped me gain solid footing as I began my life's journey. You're the best goober brothers a sister could have.

Acknowledgments

Thanks to everyone who read and commented on various drafts of Devon's Story, in particular Sheri Milburn and Dejay from my writers' group, whose advice I cherish. Another big thanks go out to Valerie Bernardin and Susana (WildLX), my French language specialists. Thanks to my other readers, Deidra Mitchell, Shirl the girl Wright, Angela Perkins, Tameca Woodall, Lori Hood, Chantal Roy, Diana Schnitzer, Joan Nelson, and Yvonne Vassel. Thanks again to Mary Phillips and J. Robin Whitley at Regal Crest for another enlightening editing experience and to Donna Pawlowski for her wonderful cover designs. Again, I must thank my very supportive family: my parents, Paul and JoAnne Clanton; my older brother, Paul Clanton, Jr. and his wife Kim Thuon, and their two children, Ian Clanton-Thuon and Adria Clanton-Thuon; my younger brother, John Clanton and his wife Melissa McCurley, my "in-laws" Joe and Mamie Weather and their son Joey Weathers. You all know that you are with me no matter how far apart we are. And thanks, finally, to my anchor, Jackie Weathers, who continues to help me learn to chill out and "worry as needs be."

Author's Note to the Revised Edition

After I retired from teaching, I have been able to do many things. One is to dig into all those books I purchased over the years but never had time to read. Another is to go back and revise my earlier works now that I'm with a new publisher.

This is a revised edition, not a second edition. Nothing major has changed in the story plot. Only the grammar, punctuation, and awkward stuff (to my current eyes and ears) have been changed, updated, or eliminated.

I must also make another note about phones and technology. When this was written in 2009, texting was just becoming a thing, and many households still had landlines. There was also no expectation for students to have their own individual computers in school. It seems odd to me now, but that's how it was aback then.

I'm hopeful that the emotions and situations will stand the test of time and that you will enjoy Devon's falling in love coming-out story.

Cheers,
Barb
Central Florida (September 2024)

Table of Contents

Chapter 1

The Luckiest Person

I didn't know how Missy managed to look so good. I mean, my sister cried as much as I did, but she still looked fresh and fabulous like those models in *Seventeen* magazine. Not that I read *Seventeen* on a regular basis—I'm just saying.

My face did that scrunched-up thing again, which meant I was about to cry. Through a haze of tears, I saw Mrs. Bordeaux barreling right for me. Damn. I must have stayed in one place too long.

"Devon, my dear." Her jiggly arm slid around my waist. "I'm so sorry for your loss. Mildred, er, your grandmother was such a wonderful person. I know how close the two of you were."

I held my breath, hoping she'd go away. Why couldn't everybody just stop trying to console me and leave me alone? I nodded without looking at her.

But Mrs. Bordeaux held on. "Mildred always talked about you at bridge. She was so proud of you and Missy, her two favorite grandchildren. Missy off at college, you doing so well in high school. In fact, just last week, she was saying..."

I couldn't listen anymore. I didn't want to hear what my grandmother was doing *just last week*, because just three days ago she was alive and breathing. I focused all my energy on holding it together while Mrs. Bordeaux rambled on. Thank God my favoritest sister in the whole world rescued me. Sometimes I couldn't believe that we were sisters because she was so pretty and I was so, I don't know, boring. Missy's long hair—she would call it chestnut—was clasped behind her head with a barrette Grandma had given her forever ago. My hair— the color of wet cardboard—hung lifelessly just below my shoulders. And I never would have been able to pull off wearing a little black dress like the one Missy had on. I was boring and plain with my black pants, button-up white shirt like Dad wore to work, and black dress shoes that pinched my toes.

"Devon," Missy said as she grabbed my hand. "I need you in the other room to look over some papers." To Mrs. Bordeaux, she said, "I hope you don't mind if I steal Devon away for a minute."

"Of course, dear." Mrs. Bordeaux released me and moved on to another victim. I almost laughed out loud when she zeroed in on my dad. I'd have to tease him about that later if I could ever figure out how to breathe without crying.

Missy led me to the front hallway, where they kept all these empty envelopes for donations, like to the ambulance corp. Yeah, they took Grandma away last Sunday in an ambulance. If I'd had any money, I would have donated, but I didn't.

"Hey, squirt. Mrs. Bordeaux sure had you, didn't she?"

"Yeah," I said. I would have said more, but my voice wasn't working too well. The only thing I could add was, "Thanks."

"No problem. Listen, if you need to get away from all of this, go down that hallway." She pointed to a narrow, dark hallway I hadn't seen before. "I saw a private bathroom and a water fountain down there. I don't think anybody knows about it, and you can be alone for a few minutes."

I nodded again. Missy could read me like a book. We were both juniors, but she was a junior at Plattsburgh State while I was a junior at Grasse River High School. She had driven home from college earlier in the day for the wake, and I got to stay home from school. Any other time, I would have loved a break from the grind of school, but a wake wasn't my idea of fun.

Missy didn't dare hug me because she knew I'd break down into a quivering mass of sobs if she did. She knew how sensitive I was about things. She just patted my arm and went back into the crowd of people. I stood alone in the hallway for several minutes, glad to be off Mrs. Bordeaux's radar. I pretended to be fascinated with the donation envelopes and pulled them out one by one, barely seeing them. When I pulled out an envelope for the Grasse River Animal Shelter, my face scrunched up again. Grandma loved the animal shelter. We went there all the time. Just me and her. We brought food for the cats and dogs and old towels, and we even walked the dogs sometimes. That was our special place. Grandpa said we were two peas in a pod when it came to

2

loving animals. Grandma and I always wanted to adopt one or two or twelve dogs and bring them home, but my mom had bad allergies, so we had to be content with seeing the dogs at the shelter.

But Grandma and I couldn't do that anymore, could we?

The sobs started deep inside. Deep inside my heart, I think. Through the sheen of tears distorting my vision, I found the shadowy hallway Missy had pointed out earlier. I shuffled down it, barely picking my feet off the plush red carpet to the blessedly empty bathroom. I went in and locked the door behind me. I hoped no one heard me because the weirdest sounds started coming from somewhere inside me. Every time I tried to catch my breath, I couldn't. I buried my face in my hands and tried to muffle the awful noises. When I finally caught my breath, I grabbed a paper towel to wipe the tears off my face. Thank God I didn't wear makeup, otherwise it would have been spread all over the place. That's why I had no idea how Missy still looked so good.

I splashed water on my face in an attempt to look presentable. I was fairly certain that my little hysterical episode qualified me to proclaim that wakes sucked. What was the point? Just to make you cry? I can do that on my own, thank you. I'd rather not cry in front of a bunch of people—most of whom I didn't know.

The bathroom door squeaked open, and I prayed the hallway would be empty. Luck was with me. I stopped at the water fountain, and before getting a drink, I took another deep breath to make sure I wasn't going to melt down again. So far, so good. I pressed the round button and watched the water make a high parabolic arc. My math teacher taught us about parabolic arcs in eighth grade. It's weird where my mind went to distract me from my grief. Too bad it didn't work, because as I leaned down to get a drink, I realized that my grandmother would never get another drink of water again. The water I had in my mouth refused to go down the right pipe, and I started choking. I doubled over, coughing, trying to get air back into my lungs.

I felt a hand on my back. "Keep coughing," the mystery voice said. "You're okay. Just keep coughing."

I did, but at the same time, I looked at the mystery woman's shoes. At least it wasn't Mrs. Bordeaux. When I caught my breath, I stood up only to peer right into the most perfect pair of dark brown eyes I'd ever seen. They matched the color of her skin, too. She was the most beautiful Black girl I'd ever seen. No, that wasn't quite right. She was the most beautiful *girl* I'd ever seen, period. But I'd seen her before. We were in the same French class. She sat in the front, and I sat in the back. I passed by her seat every day. Why hadn't I ever noticed this beautiful girl before?

"Devon, right?" she asked me.

I nodded because I still didn't have my voice yet on account of the fact that I'd just tried to inhale water and the fact that her body was way too close to mine.

"We're in the same French class. I'm Rebecca. Rebecca Washington." She flipped her ponytail behind her shoulder.

I choked out, "Devon Raines." That started another coughing fit.

"Oh, no," she whimpered and rubbed my back again. "Breathe, Devon, just breathe."

Her hand felt so good on my back. Comforting. I couldn't believe this amazing girl was paying attention to me. That was when I remembered she was just doing her job. Her family, duh, owned the Washington Funeral Home. Now, it made sense. Rebecca probably helped out after school when someone's grandmother died on them.

I started crying again; I couldn't help it. I was such a ticking time bomb that the randomest things set me off.

Rebecca seemed to want to panic but then said calmly, "Okay, okay, Devon. Look, here's what I do when I can't hold it together. Just try to take a slow and steady breath. Hold it. Good, that's good. And then exhale slowly. That's it."

I took another deep breath and held it. I didn't feel like I was going to lose it again. I'd melt down later, but right now, I had myself temporarily under control.

She smiled at me, looked right into my red-rimmed and swollen eyes, and said, "I have to breathe like that before a dance performance. I get so nervous."

I gave her as much of a smile as I could muster under the circumstances.

"Atta girl," Rebecca said and smiled with me. Her teeth shined white and bright against her dark skin.

Her glowing smile captured me like a willing prisoner. I laughed inside.

What would this amazing girl think if she knew I was into girls? What would she think if she found out I thought she was gorgeous? And what would my grandmother think? I apologized to my grandmother because this was, after all, a gathering for her benefit, not a place for me to check out girls. Not that I ever checked out girls. Not really. I figured out I was sapphicly-inclined about three and a half years ago at the end of seventh grade when I fell head over heels in love with Marcy Berger. I never told her, of course. I never told anyone. Part of trying to keep my three-and-a-half-year secret included not overtly checking out girls.

"Thanks," I said when I found my voice. "I should get back. My mom's probably wondering where I am."

"Okay." Rebecca's face softened. "I, uh, I'm sorry for your loss."

She said it so sincerely with just the right amount of sympathy in her voice that I believed she truly was sorry for my loss. She'd probably said that phrase a thousand times in her life, but I think she meant it when she said it to me.

"Thanks." I turned to go back up the dark and narrow hallway. By the time I reemerged into the well-lit room with the casket, I finally felt ready to tell my grandmother goodbye.

~~~

I kicked off my black dress shoes and flung myself on the bed. My head sank deliciously into the pillow. Yeah, wakes sucked. And the joy of this whole thing wasn't even over. In less than twelve hours, I'd be back at Washington's funeral home, trying to keep it together again for my grandmother's funeral. What fun. At least I would get out of school for another day. Being absent from school would give me an excuse to talk to Rebecca later and ask her about the French homework I missed.

As I lay on my bed, I figured I should at least get out of my black dress pants and white shirt that Missy had ironed for me. I would have been okay with the wrinkles, but she insisted. She didn't even give me a hard time about it. She just took the shirt and pants and ironed them. That's how I knew she wasn't her usual self because she always lectured me about stuff like that.

5

On Missy's side of our room, her flowery bedspread with ruffled trim made her bed look as if she never slept in it. My bed stayed in a perpetual state of undress. Who had time to make it, and what was the point? You were just going to get back in it in a few hours, anyway. Of course, now that Missy was in college, I kind of had the room to myself. This used to be just my room until Grandma moved in with us five years ago after Grandpa died. Passed away. Went to a better place. Grandpa's passing was kind of hard, too, but I think I was too young to really get it. I mean, I cried and all, but back then, my eleven-year-old self was devastated at how sad my mom and dad and Missy were. And Grandma, too. She just cried all the time. She tried to live on her own for a while, but my dad went to get her after a couple of months, and she moved into Missy's room, and Missy moved into mine.

I didn't mind. Not really. I liked my big sister. With four years between us, sibling rivalry didn't bother us too much. And besides, Missy came from a planet different from mine, anyway. She loved to fuss with her long hair, while I just threw a rubber band around mine to keep it out of my face. She loved to go to the gym. She'd do cardio twenty-four-seven if she could. I liked running, but not in front of people, not in a gym on a treadmill or on a sports team. I liked to be outside so I could breathe the air and see the trees even when it snowed.

Missy's side of the room had posters of hunky guys. She even had the New York City men's firefighters calendar on the wall. God, there was no question Missy was into guys. I wish I could get the women's version of that calendar, but that would be a total giveaway, wouldn't it? Still, when you looked at my side of the room, my side screamed gay, gay, gay because my posters were girls, girls, girls. I had posters of Melissa Etheridge, Serena and Venus Williams, and The Indigo Women—that's what I called them because they definitely weren't *girls*. Jessica Alba hung on my wall, too. Okay, to the untrained eye, they were magazine pictures of the Fantastic Four from those movies, but as far as I was concerned, they were pictures of Jessica Alba.

Even though Missy and I were as different as night and day, we did have one major thing in common. Journalism. Missy wanted to be one of those talking heads, one of those pretty news anchors who read from a teleprompter. I thought she was wasting her talent, though, because she was such a good writer, but as a junior at Plattsburgh State, more than halfway to her bachelor's degree, she should know what she wanted to do by now. I wanted to write, though, and I'd probably end up at Plattsburgh, too, because Missy told me about some cool courses in environmental and nature writing they offered there. That was right up my alley. Save the planet and all that. By the time I got to Plattsburgh, though, Missy would have graduated. I think Sunnybrook Elementary was the last school we attended at the same time, but I was too young to remember.

I looked at the bright red numbers on my alarm clock. Nine thirty. It was too late to go for a run. I sighed and made myself get up. I needed to hang up my clothes so I could wear them again for the funeral.

I pulled on a pair of sweatpants and a T-shirt. My mother hated the fact that I wore sweatpants and a t-shirt as pajamas, but there was no way in heck I was going to wear some girly nightgown. No way. She used to buy me one for Christmas every year. But that stopped a couple of years ago when I got to high school.

I turned out the overhead light and crawled into bed, even though it was kind of early. I pulled my plain, boring blue comforter all the way up to my neck and wriggled down into my nest of flannel sheets. What else could I do? Sit around and talk with them downstairs about Grandma? No, I'd had enough of that at the wake. I decided that I wasn't going to have a wake when I died. I'd have to let someone know that, though, wouldn't I? How did you go about doing something like that? Did you sit down with your children and tell them how you wanted to be buried and stuff? Did you tell them what you wanted to wear in the coffin? Did Grandma have that conversation with Dad? Did she know we were going to have the wake at Washington's Funeral Home? Did she see me from heaven crying out of control in the bathroom? Did she see Rebecca help me? Does she know I'm a lesbian now? Now that she's in heaven, can she see everything?

This time last week, Grandma was alive. Grandma was here in the house. She died on Sunday. Would Sunday the twenty-fifth of October become one of those dates I'd remember every year and cry out of control?

I wondered about the last thing Grandma had to eat. I couldn't remember what we had for dinner Sunday night. Spaghetti, maybe? I couldn't remember much except the sudden commotion downstairs that jarred me from the newspaper article I'd been writing about global warming. I leaped out of my desk chair at the shrillness in my mother's voice, asking Grandma over and over, "Are you all right? Mildred, are you all right?"

I knew Grandma wasn't all right because I heard Dad call 911. Missy wasn't home. She was in Plattsburgh. I crept down the stairs and saw my grandmother on the floor of the living room with her eyes closed and her hands clutching her chest. I couldn't make sense of it. I watched my mom kneel as if in slow motion and lean her ear over Grandma's mouth. Reality came crashing in when I recognized this from those films they made us watch in Health class in ninth grade. Horror filled my veins as Mom tilted Grandma's head back to give her CPR. Blood pounded through my head, and I couldn't hear anything anymore. I found myself on the bottom stair, even though I didn't remember moving. Dad took over the CPR while Mom leaned back and clutched both hands to her chest. At first, I thought she was having a heart attack, but then I realized she was just panicked.

When I heard the sirens, I found a purpose. I rushed over and opened up the front door. Flinging on the outside light, I called back, "Mom, I'll tell them where to come."

Mom just nodded, and I fled out the front door. I couldn't watch anymore. I knew my mom and dad were doing all they could for her. Later, after the ambulance took her and Dad away, Mom told me that Grandma had probably had a heart attack. The doctor down at Grasse River Hospital confirmed it.

I felt myself getting all jittery and tense all over again as I remembered that awful night, so I clenched my jaw tight and willed myself not to cry. I heard Missy's steps in the hallway, so I rolled over on my bed and faced the wall.

~~~

High cotton candy clouds drifted across the brilliant blue sky. Funeral weather should be cold and rainy, not bright and sunny. Definitely rainy because November started that depressing time of year in northern New York when the sun didn't come out until April or May. But, no, sunny skies like this made you want to fly kites or go swimming in the Grasse River, except for the fact that it was forty degrees. But it definitely didn't feel like a funeral day.

Rebecca must have been at school, but that didn't stop me from looking for her during the service at the funeral home. Her parents, along with Rebecca's older brother, Reggie, kept events running smoothly. Reggie had the same regal look of authority as his dad and would probably take over the family business when Mr. and Mrs. Washington retired. It looked that way, anyway. Mr. Washington was a distinguished-looking man. He even had a touch of gray in his sideburns and temples. And Mrs. Washington was as beautiful as Rebecca. Her skin was a bit darker than her husband's, and she kept her hair pulled back into a sort of tight bun low on her neck. She even had a chopstick stuck in it that held everything in place, I guess. Missy would know what that hairstyle was called, but to me, she just looked elegant. It was clear where Rebecca got her amazing looks.

During the service, I barely listened to the minister. We weren't a church kind of family, and none of us knew him, so I felt okay not listening. And besides, if I did listen, it only made me cry, and since I was trapped in the front row, I couldn't sneak out if I lost it. So, to take my mind elsewhere, I thought about Rebecca and her family. Did they live upstairs in the funeral home? That would be kind of creepy. I'd have to ask Rebecca the next time I saw her. I almost smiled because a warehouse of things to ask her filled my mind.

Occasionally, the minister's words penetrated my tough outer shell, and I felt myself getting weepy again. I knew I didn't want a repeat performance of my hysterics from the night before, so I scratched myself raw on the inside of my forearm. My head almost believed the physical pain was more important than the emotional pain. Almost.

This time, I didn't mind so much when all those people told me that my grandma was "in a better place" or they were "sorry for my loss." I didn't mind because that meant the service was o-v-e-r. I didn't even mind when Mrs. Bordeaux gave me another one of her stifling hugs.

The pallbearers moved around the casket, lifted it gently, and then inched toward the hearse. Missy was one of the pallbearers, but I was glad they didn't need me to be one because I probably would've started crying again and dropped my side on Dad's foot or something.

Mr. Washington's cousin, a policeman, turned on the flashing red lights and sirens on his motorcycle and led the hearse and the whole procession through town to the cemetery. We even got to run all the red lights. That was kind of cool—a little parade for Grandma.

I had been to Greystone Cemetery once before when we went there for Grandpa's funeral. He had died in January, and they stored him in this outdoor mausoleum place because they couldn't put him in the frozen ground. They buried him in the spring but never told us when, so thank goodness I didn't have to witness that. But the ground wasn't frozen today, and as we pulled up to the burial site, the first thing I saw was the deep, dark hole waiting to be filled. What a barbaric custom.

I got out of the backseat of the car and waited for my mom to get out of the front passenger side. We didn't talk. I wouldn't have been able to, anyway, because tears choked my throat closed again. I couldn't look at the deep hole in the ground waiting for Grandma. I know we had to bury her and all, but did we have to throw dirt on her, too? The whole thing was out of the Dark Ages or something.

Missy walked toward the hearse with my dad. Uncle Joe, my dad's younger brother, began pulling out the bright blue casket. My dad went to the other side. Missy grabbed the gold handle next to Dad while the other pallbearers grabbed theirs. I could tell the casket was heavy by the way they picked their way carefully over the grass. Mr. Washington gave them soft but precise instructions for placing the casket on the metal structure over the open grave. Mrs. Washington directed the rest of us to the rows of white chairs. I wanted to stand in the back so no one could see me cry, but Mrs. Washington ushered me to the front row, the family row.

The metal structure had this big turn crank with gears they'd use to lower Grandma into the ground. I tried to think of the whole thing with a journalist's eye, but reality kept crashing in because this was way too personal. My grandmother was in that stupid wooden box, and they were going to turn that stupid crank and lower her into the ground. There was no way I was going to throw dirt on her casket. No way. I didn't even care if it was tradition or whatever. My mouth turned into a frown all on its own. My eyes filled with tears, and I couldn't breathe very well. I looked down at my uncomfortable dress shoes and ignored my sister when she came to sit next to me. My dad sat next to my mom. I squeezed my eyes shut as the tears spilled over. I didn't wipe at them because then everyone would know I was crying. Missy knew, though, because she grabbed my hand. I couldn't look at her.

I did sneak a peek at the minister, though. I thought we were done with him. Apparently, we weren't. He started talking again about sister Mildred and her return to God. I would have lost it if Rebecca hadn't suddenly appeared behind him out of nowhere. She stood with her family off to the side. Her look of compassion would have tipped me over into hysterical land if not for the fact that she mouthed the word "breathe" to me. She took a deep breath of her own as if to show me what to do. I took a breath and held it for a second. I felt the mud in my brain recede a little. I wasn't going to blow at that moment.

The look of relief on Rebecca's face sent my heart soaring. Through my bleary eyes, I could still tell that she was beautiful. She wore black pants—Missy would have called them slacks, I guess—and an orange shirt. Okay, blouse. Her brown sweater matched her dark skin, too. She had such smooth skin. At least it looked smooth from here. My heart began beating faster. And my hands got sweaty. I hoped Missy wouldn't notice, but she'd think it was from the funeral, anyway. I wanted to touch Rebecca's cheek to see how soft it was.

I took another deep breath and apologized to my grandma again. Missy squeezed my hand. She must have thought I was crying. Actually, I was just trying to get my priorities straight.

After an eternity, the minister finished his speech, sermon, whatever it was, and then Mr. Washington thanked us all for coming and informed the crowd that they would lower the casket once everyone had gone home. I loved Mr. Washington at that moment.

As Missy and I walked back to the car, I tried to find Rebecca without making it look obvious. I stopped and mumbled something to Missy about having to tie my shoe. Missy kept going on toward the car, and I knelt down. I picked my head up and gulped when I saw Rebecca heading right for me with a bouquet of carnations in her arms. I jumped up, leaving my shoelace undone. I smoothed my hair back and then felt like an idiot.

11

"These," Rebecca said, handing the flower arrangement to me, "are the last of them."

I took the colorful bouquet and walked them over to the backseat. "Thanks."

"No problem." She smiled at me in that sympathetic way that made my stomach clench. I knew I should say something, but I couldn't get my brain in gear, so I looked at my shoes while the silence between us grew to awkward proportions.

Rebecca spoke first. "Well, I guess I'll see you at school." She turned to go.

"Okay," I choked out. But then my brain finally engaged, and I called after her, "Rebecca?"

She turned. "Yeah?"

"Thanks for the breathing lessons."

Her eyes lit up like the fourth of July. Her smile was so big you'd think I just told her she'd won the lottery. "No problem, Devon. I've had a little experience." She gestured toward the hearse.

"Yeah, I guess you have."

"I have to finish up here, but I'll see you in French tomorrow, okay?"

The rest of the world disappeared at that moment, and through my grief, I allowed myself a moment of selfishness to drink in her soft brown eyes. They were smiling at me—okay, maybe from sympathy, but still—her eyes were smiling at *me*.

I swallowed hard and said, "*Oui, oui, mademoiselle. À demain.*" French had just become my favorite class. There was no way I was going to ask my mom if I could stay home now because out of the shadow of my grandmother's death, a tiny flame had ignited in my heart.

Chapter 2

Back at School

The words on the computer swam in front of my eyes. Even though I had gone to bed right after the funeral, I didn't sleep much and could hardly keep my eyes open at school. I looked out the classroom window over the top of my computer onto a drizzly cold October Friday.

In the reflection of the window, I watched my journalism teacher, Mrs. Gibson, lean over Mike Reynolds' shoulder and point at something on his computer screen. Apparently, Mike didn't know how to structure a newspaper article. The long chain from Mrs. Gibson's bifocals rested on his shoulder as she reminded him patiently, in her impatient way, about putting the attention-grabbing details in the first paragraph. She told him not to give away the whole farm but just enough to hook the reader. Evidently, Mrs. Gibson was in another one of her moods. It was one of those moods where her students couldn't do anything right.

Both Mike and I had taken Journalism I the year before as sophomores, and we knew how to structure an article. And, besides, as boys' sports editor, how could he not know how to put a story together? I smiled to myself because As Mrs. Gibson scolded him, he looked like a little boy with his downcast gaze and short blonde crew cut. Even his "Yes, ma'am" was boyish. I liked Mike, but not in that way. I think he liked me, too, *in* that way. A lot of girls would probably go for his lean runner's body, but not me. After all, I hadn't been straight since seventh grade, and I probably wasn't even straight then but hadn't known it.

All the journalism courses were essentially geared toward producing the bimonthly student newspaper—the Grasse River High School Gazette. The September/October issue came out in October, and now we were getting the

November/December issue ready. Of course, my article on the environment was late since it had been due two days ago, the day of Grandma's wake.

I tried, once again, to focus on the words on my computer screen. My dad's company, Alum Castings, was one of the biggest employers in northern New York, and they had just begun a series of environmental projects. One of the projects—the one I was trying to write about—proposed to replant thousands of black ash trees in the wetlands. This was the same article I'd been working on the Sunday Grandma died. No wonder I couldn't finish it. I closed my eyes and gave up with a sigh.

I opened my eyes when I heard Mrs. Gibson approaching. My fingers hit the keyboard, and I started typing some nonsense about the benefits of the Black Ash tree to the Northern New York environment. I'd go back and delete it later, but I had to look busy. Mrs. Gibson stood right behind me, but my fingers typed away furiously as I pretended to be thoroughly engrossed in my article.

"Devon," she said in her shrill voice. "I see you're busy, but let me interrupt you for a second."

"Okay," I said, but kept my eyes on the screen for a moment more and finished my made-up sentence. I hit the period on the keyboard hard as if to finish an important thought and then swiveled in my chair to face her.

"I know you've been out for a few days—sorry for your loss—and I'll let you settle in today, but on Monday, we need to talk about your future with the newspaper. Okay?"

My future? What did she mean by that? What was I supposed to say? I simply said, "Okay."

She tapped my shoulder once and then headed to her next victim.

I had never been late with an article before. In fact, I usually turned them in early. How could she question my future with the newspaper? Out of the corner of my eye, I saw Mike looking at me. His closed-lipped smile and sympathetic puppy dog eyes were more than I could take at that moment, so I turned away and rubbed the bridge of my nose. I wanted to go home but knew I couldn't because I had to survive long enough to make it all the way to eighth-period French. Rebecca would be there. How many stupid times had I seen Rebecca at school and never noticed her?

~~~

The drizzling rain had pretty much stopped by lunchtime, so Gail and I braved the damp cold and ate outside. We commandeered one of the six round tables under the overhang. Seniors were allowed to leave campus for lunch, so by default, the cafeteria courtyard was the unofficial juniors' domain. The fenced-in area constantly reminded us of our lower status, but I didn't care. Hanging out there made us feel like the top dogs of the school.

I had already braced the long lines and gotten my usual turkey sandwich and fruit cup. Most of the other kids got french fries or chips, but greasy food never sat well on my stomach, so I always tried something healthier. And ditching the greasy stuff helped keep my acne under control. Missy would approve.

Gail sat down next to me and opened her brown bag lunch. Gail Marsters had been my best friend ever since the fourth grade when we got put in Mrs. Johnson's class together. Old Mrs. Johnson assigned us as reading partners, and ever since then, we'd been as thick as thieves. At least, that's how my mom referred to us. In middle school, Gail weighed about ninety pounds, so I used to think I was fat at a hundred and ten. But Missy helped me understand that Gail and I just had different body types. Still, I took up jogging just to be sure, and I still run because I feel good when I do. Gail and I have practically the same hair, too. Plain old brown and shoulder length, but Gail always managed to make her hair look good with barrettes and clips and bands. I couldn't be bothered with that stuff except when I went running. That's when I'd throw a rubber band around it or throw on my Plattsburgh Cardinals baseball hat.

Gail pulled out a sandwich from her paper bag and sighed.

I looked over. Peanut butter and jelly. "Your brother made the lunches again?"

"Phht," she spat. "I can't wait until it's my turn. Oh well. Trade?"

"Halvies. Not full. Full when you have tuna fish or roast beef." I smiled at her, and she smiled back in that best friend sort of way. Her smile said we were in this together, through thick and thin. I gave her half my turkey sandwich in exchange for an overly peanut butter-laden sandwich.

15

Gail held my gaze a bit longer than usual. Uh oh, something was up. Before I could ask her where her boyfriend Joey was, she asked me softly, "So how'd it go yesterday?"

Yesterday. The funeral. It came flooding back so fast that my heart broke all over again before I could stop it. I closed my eyes and looked away. Before I let myself get too choked up, I managed to mutter, "It went okay." I sighed and added, "As far as those things go."

"Yeah, I know." She rubbed my back over my jean jacket. "I know. I'm sorry I couldn't go. I wanted to be there, you know that, right? But my mom wanted me in school." She continued to rub my jean jacket.

"I know." I did know. I pushed my lunch away. Food kind of turned my stomach at that point.

Joey, Gail's boyfriend of about three months, came bounding up to the table out of breath. He was a definite hottie. He kept his short black hair neat and trimmed, unlike a lot of the other guys around school who looked like they'd never been introduced to a comb.

Gail's face lit up when she saw him. He threw his backpack on the damp gravel and sat down. It wasn't hard to tell that they really liked each other. He leaned over for a kiss from Gail which she gave freely. I felt a little pervy watching them, so I looked away.

I looked out past the maple trees in the courtyard, past the cars in the senior parking lot, and the tall pines separating the school's property from the neighborhood behind. Storm clouds hurried past us in the dark sky on their way toward Canada.

An elbow jammed into my side, jolting me out of my sky-gazing. "Hey." I scowled at Gail. She pointed to Joey.

Joey said, "Hey, Devon, sorry about your grandma. Funerals suck, don't they?"

I laughed. "Yeah, they do." Bless Joey for knowing the right thing to say. "Thanks," I added.

I looked back to the changing sky and inhaled the scent of the damp maple leaves scattered around the courtyard. I even got a faint whiff of pine and wondered if my grandma was up there in that tumultuous sky. Was she with Grandpa and Great-aunt Bertie? I felt the now-familiar sting of tears in my eyes and was amazed that I had any more tears to give. My chest tightened, and I knew this could go one of two ways. I might be able to sit here crying quietly, or I might have another complete meltdown like the one I'd had at the funeral home.

I used the clean napkin from Gail's lunch to wipe at my nose when, all of a sudden, loud voices interrupted my misery. To my amazement, Rebecca burst into the courtyard with her friends. Jessie Something-or-other, one of Rebecca's friends, was telling a loud story about something that happened to her brother. Jessie played on the girls' basketball team, but I was glad that I didn't play basketball because she was kind of mean and scary-looking. I didn't know a lot about Jessie, but I'd never seen her smile. Okay, maybe I'd seen an evil grin or something, but not a genuine smile. She had hundreds of tiny braids in her hair. I would have to ask Missy, but I think they were called corn rows or something. The braids hung down almost to her shoulders and looked nice against her white shirt and dark skin. I couldn't remember the name of their other friend, but I think she played on the basketball team, too.

Watching Rebecca with her friends lifted me out of my funk a little. As I thought about it, I realized that those three hung out together all the time at lunch, just like Gail, Joey, and me. I sort of never realized it before now, but all the Black kids seemed to hang out in one big group. Jessie's story must have been mesmerizing because Rebecca didn't see me at all. I took that opportunity to watch her. I tried not to make it obvious like I was a stalker chick or something. She wore her hair pulled back in that cool-looking bun that her mother wore at the wake, but Rebecca had a pencil in it instead of a chopstick. The exposed curve of her neck definitely caught my attention. Yeah, maybe I was a stalker. She had on black capri pants and wore the tiniest shoes I'd ever seen. They looked like dancer's shoes or something. For some reason, I didn't think Rebecca played on the basketball team, but the purple and white Grasse River basketball sweatshirt she wore made me wonder.

I took a deep breath when reality came, waltzing in again uninvited. We buried Grandma yesterday. I looked down at the uneaten sandwich halves in front of me and tried to swallow the enormous lump growing in my throat. I wished the stupid bell would ring so I could go to class and have something else to think about. I looked up, hoping to catch another glimpse of Rebecca, and to my surprise, she was staring right at me. I gulped. Her smile brightened my heart and traveled down to my toes and back again. I smiled back. I couldn't help it.

Rebecca mouthed to me, "Are you okay?"

I shrugged my shoulders and rolled my eyes.

She nodded in sympathy and mouthed the word, "Breathe."

I nodded and couldn't help grinning. I mouthed, "Thank you" across the courtyard, and this time *her* smile got bigger.

I wanted to get up and talk to her, but Rebecca looked away from me just as Jessie turned back toward her. I got the distinct feeling that Rebecca didn't want Jessie to see her talking to me. As their conversation continued, I realized I must have been staring at them because Jessie challenged me with her eyes as if warning me to mind my own business. I looked away quickly, sure she had been able to read my thoughts.

Gail nudged me in the side again. We were going to have to talk about all this side-nudging soon. I gave her my best "What do you want now?" glare.

"Who's that?" She nodded her head toward Rebecca.

"Oh, she's just—her family owns the funeral home, and she helped me get through it yesterday."

"That was nice of her."

Oh, but there was so much more, like the steady flame warming my heart and all those forbidden thoughts swirling around my head. I always thought that Gail and I were as close as twins, and we kind of were, except when it came to certain things. Certain things like the fact that Gail would rather go out with somebody named Joey or Travis or Michael while I would rather go out with somebody named Rebecca or Ashley or Mia. But Gail did not know any of this, and I wasn't sure I was ever going to tell her.

~~~

I lay on my bed, throwing Grizzly, my stuffed teddy bear, into the air and catching him. I'm sure he didn't appreciate it, but throwing him around helped me chill out after the longest day of school ever. Except for those times I got to see Rebecca, of course. She smiled at me again in French. I wanted to talk to her after class, but by the time I got my books jammed into my backpack, she was already on her way out the door. At least she turned around and said, "See ya, Devon."

I said, "See ya," right back. *See ya.* Yeah, I wanted to see her. I wanted to go out with her. What was the difference between seeing someone and going out with someone? I'd have to ask Missy.

I threw Grizzly in the air again and then held him tight when I remembered about Jessie. Rebecca's friend Jessie had been waiting for her right outside the door to the classroom. How Jessie had gotten there so fast was beyond me.

I threw Grizzly in the air again just as Missy walked into our room.

"Hey, squirt," she said, smiling. "Why are you torturing Grizzly?" I moved over so she could sit on the edge of the bed.

"He's okay with it. Really." I grinned at her but hugged Grizzly to my chest instead of throwing him again.

"How was school today?"

I sighed. "Long."

"I'm sure, but now you have the whole weekend to regroup."

"That's true. When are you going back to Plattsburgh?"

"Sunday. After dinner." Missy usually went back right after lunch, but I think this time, she didn't want to leave the family. We all had a lot of "regrouping" to do.

"Cool." We sat in silence for a moment. I wanted to ask her so many things, but I didn't know where to start. Then I remembered Mrs. Gibson from the first period of journalism. "Mrs. Gibson was on my case today."

"Uh, oh. Was she in one of her moods?"

"Yeah." I laughed. "She had those moods when you were in her class?"

"Oh, yeah. No one was safe. Not even Missy Raines, editor-in-chief."

"Really? Not even you?" That I could not believe. Mrs. Gibson thought the sun rose and set around Missy.

"Yeah, even me. But whatever she's on your case about probably isn't too earth-shattering. What did she say?"

"My environment article was due Wednesday—"

"The one about Dad's company?"

"Yeah, and I still couldn't finish it. You know, because..." I gestured toward Grandma's room.

Missy's eyes softened. "Mm hmm."

"And Mrs. Gibson came by during class while I was working on it and said something like, 'Let's talk about your *future* with the newspaper.'" I used air quotes around the word future. "Can you believe it? I've never been late with an article before. In fact—" I poked the air with my finger, "I've even rewritten articles that other people have messed up. It's not fair."

"And she sounded serious? Never mind, I'm sure she was. I know how she can get when she gets something in her head. Well, I suggest you finish your article and make sure it's absolutely pristine. And make a point of uploading it right at the beginning of the period on Monday."

"Yeah, I will. I have no life anyway. I'm home on a Friday night, aren't I?"

"What's Gail doing?"

"Oh, she has Joey now, so she doesn't need me tagging along all the time. Fifth wheel and all."

"Oh, Devon. There's somebody out there for you."

"Phht." I rolled my eyes. "Sure there is."

"Devon!" She smacked my leg playfully. "Stop that. With that attitude, no one will ever be interested. Is there anybody on your mind?"

How could she ask me that question? She had radar better than Mom's. She couldn't know, could she? I felt myself blush.

When I didn't answer, she said quietly, "Devon, look, whoever they are would have to be crazy not to want to go out with you."

"Thanks, but you're my sister. You're not qualified to judge." I stuck my tongue out at her in a most mature manner.

She didn't go for the bait but said, "Listen, you're a beautiful girl. Smart and funny. Have you called them?"

That was the second time Missy used the plural pronoun. They. Them. As a journalist, Missy knew the difference between the words "them" and "him." Missy knew grammar. My eyes got wider when I realized that Missy knew. Missy knew I was gay. Somehow, she had figured it out.

I stammered, "Uh, no. It's just a new thing."

Missy pulled the scrunchie out of her hair and shook her head to let her

20

hair flow free. We had the same parents, but Missy got the great hair, the great looks, the great everything. I got nothing. I didn't mean to, but I sighed.

"What's the matter, squirt?"

"My hair sucks."

She reached over and looked at the ends. "Your hair looks great. No split ends. Nice and shiny."

I laughed. "You mean I have a nice coat?"

"No!" She smacked my leg playfully again. "You take care of yourself, and it shows, dufus."

I hadn't thought about this in a long time, but I mustered up the courage and asked, "Missy, can you put those highlights in my hair again?"

"The auburn tint? Oh, like we did last summer?"

"Yeah."

"Sure, I think I still have a box around here. C'mon." She got up and practically ran to the bathroom.

When I got into the bathroom, Missy looked at me with a hand on her hip. She narrowed her eyes, shook the box of hair color, and asked, "Does this have anything to do with your *new thing*?"

I know I turned red. I could feel my cheeks getting hot. "Shut up, Missy."

She just laughed and opened the box of hair color.

Chapter 3

Sports Editor

I pulled my hood up against the morning cold. I hated walking to school in the dark, but I only lived about a half mile away, so the walk wasn't too bad. Once winter hit for real it would be a different story. If I ever got a car, I'd pick up Gail on the other side of town, and then we'd get Joey. We'd all get to school warm and dry every day. But then again, Joey already had his license, which made me wonder why he and Gail didn't pick me up every morning. I'd have to talk to Gail about this oversight.

Mother Nature had great timing as the sky lightened up just as I walked through the main doors of the high school. I didn't stop at my locker, which I usually do, but went straight to Journalism with my environment article ready to upload into the November/December folder. Missy helped me edit the final copy over the weekend before she left to go back to school, so at least Mrs. Gibson wouldn't be able to give me grief about bad copy. If she wanted me to drop the course or something for the second semester, then at least I would know I had tried my best.

I picked my head up high, yanked off my hood, and readied myself for Mrs. Gibson's assessment of my future with the newspaper. I placed my backpack on the table next to my assigned computer and got out the flash drive that held my article. Mike was already there logging in. At least he had a future. As the boys' sports editor, Mrs. Gibson was probably grooming him for editor-in-chief for next year. She rarely appointed juniors as department editors, so she must have had a lot of faith in him. Too bad she had it out for me. I sighed and turned on my computer.

I saved my article on the school's network just as the bell rang to start the class. Mrs. Gibson clapped her hands twice for attention. I swiveled my seat around for our Monday morning staff meeting.

"Give me your attention." Mrs. Gibson waited until the twenty or so students turned in their chairs to face her. I always wondered if she ever got headaches from how tightly her gray hair was pulled back into her power bun.

She held the clipboard in front of her and peered down through her bifocals. "Your articles that were due last Wednesday will be edited, as usual, by the Journalism III class this week. On Thursday, you can start your rewrites. In the meantime, you need to pick new topics from the list posted on the bulletin board."

I didn't know if it was my imagination, but I could have sworn that Mrs. Gibson glared at me over her glasses when she mentioned the Wednesday deadline. The deadline I had missed.

Mrs. Gibson put her clipboard down and continued. "The November/December issue is jammed packed. The sports reports are going to take up a lot of space with fall sports wrap-ups and winter sports previews." She looked at Mike. "I assume you've received all the articles from your reporters on time?"

"Yes, ma'am. I've already started editing."

She shot him an approving glance. "Now, on to a more serious matter." She turned to look at me. "Devon—" She looked down at her clipboard as if trying to find her place. Maybe she didn't want to make direct eye contact with me when she kicked me out of the class. I could feel the other students looking at me. I swallowed hard to dislodge the sudden lump in my throat, and I practically held my breath, waiting for the guillotine to fall.

"Oh, here it is. Devon, I hinted on Friday that we needed to discuss your future."

Here comes the axe.

"Melissa Cox is moving in…." She looked back down at her clipboard. "At the end of the week. I didn't realize it was so soon."

I had no idea what Melissa Cox had to do with me, but I kept my eyes on Mrs. Gibson.

She peered at me over her glasses. "I want you to think about taking her place as girls' sports editor."

My eyes flew wide open. Editor? I wasn't getting dropped from the class?

23

I'm sure the relief showed on my face, but before I could answer, Mrs. Gibson held up her hand to stop my response. "Devon, I don't want your answer yet. Talk it over with Mike. He can tell you what the job entails, but I would like your answer by the end of the day. Fair enough?"

Fair? Absolutely. I nodded and said, "Yes, ma'am," way too enthusiastically, but how could I *not* take an editor position? So what if I had never played a single sport at Grasse River High School? That wouldn't stop me. Three minutes earlier, I thought I would need to find another class to take during first period, but she just wanted to promote me. Why didn't she just say that on Friday?

She ended the staff meeting, and I slumped back in my chair with a sigh of relief. I didn't have a moment to let my promotion sink in because Mike whipped his chair next to mine, so close, in fact, that our arms touched.

"Congrats, Devon." He held out his hand. "You'll make a great editor."

I shook his hand and hoped he couldn't feel mine trembling. "Thanks. I had no idea." I let go of his hand, but he held onto mine longer than necessary. I pretended to scoot my chair a little closer to my computer, but all I really wanted to do was move my arm away from his.

"You'll be fine. Do you want a rundown of what you have to do? *If* you take the job, that is."

I knew in my heart of hearts that I'd accept the position, but I would take the day to weigh the pros and cons. Cons? What cons?

"Sure, tell me what I'm in for, but don't scare me off, okay?"

He winked at me and then smiled in such a way that was supposed to melt my heart or something. I couldn't tell him that somebody had already beaten him to it. And what sucked was that I couldn't even tell her how I felt. That was a problem. And Mike seemed to be turning into another problem for me. Why was life getting so complicated all of a sudden? I felt my shoulders tense up even more as he outlined the many and varied duties of a sports editor. First, I had to find out who the girls' sports reporters were and what sports they covered. Most would come from the Journalism I class—the sophomores—not our class. Next, I had to get their articles, which were probably already in Melissa's network folder, and then edit, edit, edit. Mike said fixing bad writing was a tough gig, but he told me to ask him if I needed help being diplomatic. And apparently, I had more articles to edit than Mike did. The girls had seven sports in the fall—volleyball, soccer, tennis, golf, cheerleading, cross-country, and field hockey, while the guys only had five—football, golf, soccer, volleyball, and cross-country. And just when I thought the editor's job wouldn't be too taxing, Mike complicated matters by pointing out that each sport also had a junior varsity team. He moved his seat closer to me again and then further added to my workload by reminding me that each of the winter sports needed a preview for the upcoming issue. I took a deep breath and subtly moved my chair away from him again. Not only did the girls' sports editing job sound colossal, but on top of that, the boys' sports editor was coming on to me big time. What was I getting myself into?

~~~

I claimed a table inside the cafeteria in the corner near the doors to the back courtyard. The temperature hadn't gone up much since my early morning walk, and we'd probably have to eat inside from now on until the earth thawed out again in April.

I bit into my turkey sandwich while I kept an eye out for Gail and Joey. I stood up and waved my arms when they walked into the cafeteria holding hands. Gail waved back when she saw me. Joey headed to the food line while Gail made her way to me with her brown bag lunch.

"Too cold?" Gail gestured to the courtyard.

"Yeah." I pushed my backpack closer to the wall so she could pull out the chair next to me.

"Devon, your hair! I love it!"

At first, I didn't know what she was talking about, but then I remembered the auburn highlights. I reached up and brushed the hair out of my eyes. "Missy helped me."

"Oh. Missy was home?"

I tried not to let my heart react. Gail had forgotten that my grandma died eight days ago.

"Oh God, Devon." She put her hand on my forearm. "I'm sorry. I forgot. I didn't mean..." Her face turned scarlet.

"It's cool. Don't worry about it."

"Okay, but I'm sorry."

And she *was* sorry. I knew it. I felt the familiar knotting of my stomach again. *No*, I thought to myself, *there will be no more crying in public.* At home, in my room, that's where any and all crying would happen.

I sighed and unwrapped my sandwich. Gail sighed, too, when she opened yet another peanut butter and jelly sandwich. I pushed half of my sandwich toward her and said, "Halvsies?"

The smile on her face told me she knew she was forgiven. "Yeah, thanks." She picked up the half sandwich and took a bite.

She slid half her PB and J over. I gulped down a sugary, peace-making bite and then took a long drink from my water bottle.

When Joey showed up at the table, Gail grabbed his arm, relief clearly showing on her face.

I looked away from them and scanned the cafeteria for Rebecca. The Black kids usually sat together on the same side we did, but closer to the front doors, about four tables away. I saw Jessie first. Well, the back of Jessie, that is. Her solid frame and dark braids weren't hard to miss. She stood up and looked my way for an excruciatingly long time before heading toward the food line. It was as if she knew where I was the whole time. I shook off my paranoia and looked for Rebecca. I had a clear view now that Jessie was gone. The noisy cafeteria held no distractions for me as I drank in her smile, her high cheekbones, soft eyes, and dancer's grace. Her hair fell in wisps in front of her shoulders. She usually wore her hair up, but seeing her hair down made my insides twist around in a tickly sort of way.

Rebecca must have felt my eyes on her because she turned from her conversation and caught my gaze. I had a quick moment of panic because I felt like a peeping Tom, peeping Mary, whatever, but thank goodness, her smile never wavered. I automatically smiled back, hoping she couldn't see my face turn red from across the room. She gestured to her hair, which confused me for a second, and then she mouthed the words, "I like it." The highlights. She had noticed.

"Thanks," I mouthed back.

We continued to smile at each other across the four tables until Rebecca

26

looked up at Jessie, who had come back with an ice cream bar. Rebecca didn't look my way again, and it felt like somebody had turned the lights out.

"Hey," Gail said.

Her voice startled me back to my own table.

"What happened with Mrs. Gibson this morning?"

I hoped Gail hadn't seen me smiling at Rebecca, but why should that bother me? Rebecca was just another kid at school, except for the fact that I kind of melted down whenever I looked at her. Yeah, maybe that had something to do with it.

I cleared my throat and said, "Well, I wasn't tossed off the paper if that's why you're asking." I grinned wide.

"Excellent, excellent. So, what *did* happen?"

"She promoted me to girls' sports editor."

"Get out!" Gail dropped her sandwich on her lunch bag and turned to face me. "That's awesome." She leaned over and hugged me. I hugged her back but hoped Rebecca wasn't watching. I didn't want her to think that Gail was my girlfriend or anything. But, then again, that was ridiculous. The chance that Rebecca was family, a member of the church, a card-carrying member of the sapphic society was microscopic. I shook my head to get out the cobwebs.

"Um, Devon?"

"Yeah?"

"What do you know about sports?"

I laughed. "Not a thing."

"That's what I thought." Gail pulled away and turned to Joey. "Can you believe that? Sports editor?"

Joey smiled. "That's cool. When do you start?"

"Today, I guess. I have to tell Mrs. Gibson after school that I'm going to do it."

Joey asked me why Mrs. Gibson promoted me in the middle of the year, so I told them about Melissa Cox moving and how Mike Reynolds offered to help me get started. I almost choked on the last bite of my sandwich when Gail blurted out, "You should ask him out."

"What?"

"Mike Reynolds. You should ask him out. He's cute, and he's so nice. I have English with him."

I raised my eyebrows at her in disbelief, but she just shrugged and said, "You need to be in a relationship. It's about time you had somebody."

I couldn't think of a single thing to say except *Yeah, and she's sitting about four tables that way.*

~~~

The lesson on conjugating the subjunctive was apparently finished for the class period because Madame Depardieu put the dry-erase marker onto the whiteboard tray and walked to her desk. When she picked up a stack of papers, I groaned. Worksheets. I hated worksheets.

"*Votre attention, s'il vous plaît.*" Mme Depardieu started counting out enough papers for each row. "Please get zis permission slip signed right away. We are going to zee power dam on zeh St. Lawrence River. We go zeh day before Thanksgiving vacation."

I laughed in relief. They weren't worksheets. Mme Depardieu was a short, stout woman with long black hair sprinkled with gray. She wore her hair tied back every day, but by the time eighth period rolled around, loose sprigs of hair sprang everywhere. I had seen her once before school and almost didn't recognize her because her hair had been so neat.

Rebecca sat in the front row of the classroom while I sat in the back. Rebecca took the stack of permission slips from their teacher and turned all the way around in her seat to pass them to the girl sitting behind her. I didn't want to seem stalkerish, so I kept my gaze on Mme Depardieu, but I smirked in triumph when Rebecca looked my way. At least, I think she looked at me. It might have been wishful thinking, but I couldn't help the perma-grin creeping onto my face. My grin screamed so loudly that I could barely hear Mme Depardieu talking about her favorite Frenchmen, Jacques Cartier and André Masséna. I laughed to myself. Didn't she know that we'd all been to the Power Dam before? The entire fourth grade at Sunnybrook Elementary School took an annual pilgrimage to the Seaway in Massena. We went to the Eisenhower Lock and then to the Power Dam during our unit on the history of St. Lawrence County. Of course, the best part of that trip in fourth grade was when we went to the Dairy Queen afterward, and Sam Ogden got a sundae dumped on his head. My teacher Miss Wurther was so pissed, and I don't think she ever found out who did it. And to this day, I'm not even sure who did.

Mme Depardieu called for attention again. "Please get zee parent signatures right away." Her Québec accent was thick, but by this time in the school year, I could understand just about everything she said in English. "You'll miss periods one through four, and we'll be back sometime during period five. You should bring your lunch wiz you in case we're delayed getting back." This elicited a few groans from my classmates, but as long as Gail's brother didn't make my lunch, I'd be okay.

I wondered slyly if I could get my mom or dad to write me a note excusing me from the trip. I could work on the newspaper instead. I had a feeling girls' sports at Grasse River High School were going to take over my life. Wait! What was I thinking? Rebecca would be on the field trip. Forget it. A field trip with Rebecca was way better than editing.

I tucked the slip into my assignment book and wrote in the little Monday square allocated for French, "Get Permission Slip Signed Tonight!!!!" I put four exclamation points and even put a little smiley face in the square.

With only a couple of minutes left in the period, Mme Depardieu let us pack up and walk around the classroom. We couldn't leave until the bell rang, so I put my assignment book into my backpack and dared to look toward Rebecca. She zipped up her own pack and then abruptly stood up and headed toward me in the back of the room. I found myself leaning back in my chair, almost trying to get away.

Rebecca smiled when she reached me. "Your hair looks great, Devon. It brings out your pretty brown eyes."

I gulped but hoped she hadn't seen it. I knew my cheeks must have been turning red because I felt my face get hot all of a sudden. "Thanks, my sister did it for me."

"Oh, I saw your sister at the..."

She didn't finish her sentence, but I knew she was going to say "funeral." I just nodded and then dropped my head. I had to say something, but I got that choked-up feeling again. I just said, "Yeah."

She kneeled next to me and put a hand on my shoulder. "You're okay, Devon. Just breathe, okay?"

I almost melted at the compassion in her eyes. And my pulse raced so fast that I thought I would pass out. Rebecca Washington's hand rested on my shoulder—I almost couldn't deal with it, but I took a deep breath and nodded to her, saying that I was okay.

The bell was going to ring in a matter of seconds, but I couldn't think of a single thing to say, and I desperately didn't want to leave our conversation hanging on my grandmother's funeral.

I could see her look of sympathy out of the corner of my eye. She said, "Are you okay?"

"Yeah. I'm doing a lot of *breathing* these days."

She laughed. My heart melted inside my chest. I had just made Rebecca laugh.

"It works, doesn't it?" She took her hand off my shoulder, and the spot felt distractingly cold.

Without much thought, I blurted, "I'm the new girls' sports editor for the Gazette." Okay, it wasn't a smooth transition, but at least my brain had come up with something to say.

"Congratulations. You could use a distraction about now, couldn't you?"

I nodded. What she didn't know, and what no one else knew either, was that *she* was becoming my main distraction.

"You know, Devon, I'm good friends with Jessie Crowler. She's the captain of the basketball team, and I could ask her to talk to you if you want. I don't know, like an interview or something?"

"Absolutely. I have to set up a winter sports preview for basketball, so, yeah, that'd be cool."

"Great. I'll ask her." She patted my shoulder again.

The bell rang, so she stood up and headed back up the aisle. I watched Rebecca's back as she left the classroom. She moved so gracefully. As she opened the door, I saw Jessie leaning against the wall. Just before they walked off together, Jessie turned her head and sneered at me. My fists clenched. For a second, I couldn't place the reason for my instant anger until I realized what it was. Jealousy. And I had it bad.

Chapter 4

Frenglish

By Thursday morning, I felt like I'd been the girls' sports editor for two weeks instead of two days. My training with Melissa Cox after school on Tuesday and Wednesday had been rapid and intense. She had been the sports editor for only two months, but she showed me so much in those two afternoons that I knew I could do the job okay. And, besides, I could always call up Missy for advice. She was connected to her cell phone. And I had Mike, too, a few computers away. In fact, I already had a question for him. I just hoped he didn't take my attention the wrong way.

I scooted my chair toward him.

"Hang on," he said and put one finger in the air. He finished typing a sentence about the wrestling team. "Okay, what's up?" He looked at me as if my question was the most important thing in the world to him at that moment. That, of course, made me feel like a jerk for not liking him more than a friend.

I cleared my throat and said, "I emailed all the girls' sports reporters about their fall wrap-ups. So that's done. But should I go to the fall sports banquet on the Monday before Thanksgiving?"

"Yes, yes, yes. Mrs. Gibson told me that the reporters are usually on the team. I'm the boys' cross-country reporter since I'm on the team, but she said they tend to get caught up with the dinner and forget details like what place they came in or who made the all-county team."

"Pretty major."

"No kidding. So, yeah, you should go. The boys' banquet is the next night, and I'll be going to that."

"Cool. You know I'll have more questions, don't you?"

31

"Anytime. I'm glad to help."

As I scooted back to my station, I noticed out of the corner of my eye that Mike continued to watch me. I pretended not to notice and made a mental note to try and get answers from other people, even if I had to ask Mrs. Gibson because I didn't want to give him false hope. I pulled out my assignment book. In the Thursday square under Journalism, I wrote, "Go to Gym Today. Sign up for BQT." I'd probably go to the PE office right after school.

Mrs. Gibson began her daily patrol, so I jammed my assignment book in my backpack and clicked open the girls' sports folder. The varsity and junior varsity wrap-ups for four sports—cheerleading, volleyball, cross-country, and soccer—were complete. The junior varsity golf article was finished, but the varsity article was on hold because they had to make up a match against Tupper Lake on Saturday. David Pitone, the golf reporter, promised to get the article in the folder on Monday. I had plenty of articles to read over the weekend, so I told him that Monday would be soon enough. I hoped, though, that I wouldn't have to get all mean and bossy if his article was late.

Mrs. Gibson hovered behind me. "Devon, are the editor passwords working all right for you?"

"Yes, thank you. I just need the articles for varsity golf and varsity field hockey."

"Oh, field hockey," she said with an exasperated sigh. "That team is never done by the deadline. I assume they made the playoffs again?"

"Yes. Playoffs start next week." The field hockey team was Grasse River's most accomplished team. They probably had as many trophies for field hockey down in the gym as Mrs. Gibson had journalism trophies in her classroom. She even had trophies dating as far back as 1980.

"Well, if they're not done by press time, you'll have to finish the article with an editor's note."

I felt powerful all of a sudden. "What should it say?"

"Something along the lines of 'The Field Hockey team had not completed its season by press time.'"

But I hoped the team would be done, not that I wanted them to lose in the playoffs or anything, but I just wanted my first issue to be good.

"Melissa Cox said you caught on rather quickly."

I nodded. "She showed me everything. I didn't realize how much an editor did."

"A lot of hard work goes into putting out a newspaper, Devon. It's not all glamour and glitz."

I almost laughed out loud. Glamour and glitz? I held back a smile. "Yeah, I'm learning that." I turned back to my computer, and Mrs. Gibson continued her patrolling.

I had only been an editor for two days, but I wanted my first issue to be perfect. I guess I caught that disease from Missy. She would stay up late at night on the computer in our room. I used to complain about it, but eventually, I just turned toward the wall and put a pillow over my head so I could sleep. I guess it would be me at the computer late at night now.

Besides the fall wrap-ups, I also needed to get previews of winter sports. Mike told me I should highlight the girls' basketball team because they were supposed to go all the way to the state tournament this year. Of course, thinking about the basketball team made me think about Rebecca. And that, unfortunately, made me think about how stupidly jealous I had gotten over Jessie on Monday. They were probably friends, just like Gail and I were friends. No big deal, right? But I had to be careful because I didn't want to scare Rebecca off by being frosty to her friends, even though Jessie, who, for whatever reason, didn't seem to like me very much.

At least Rebecca smiled at me every day. And every day, she asked me if I was okay. I wasn't sure how I'd answer her later on today because exactly one week ago, we buried my grandmother.

But wallowing in the one-week anniversary of my grandmother's burial would have to wait. I had articles to edit. I clicked open the one about volleyball and started reading. After two paragraphs of run-on sentences, misspelled words, missing commas, and dangling prepositions, I sighed and realized editing might be tougher than I thought. The reporters were the ones who were supposed to fix the text, but it was my job to find a way to help them do that. Somehow, I'd have to find a subtle way to convey the finer points of grammar to the sophomore who had written the article. Although that didn't sound like fun, I was glad for the distraction.

~~~

It took all day, but my eighth-period French class finally arrived. And when Rebecca walked in, she hesitated at her desk in the front but then walked right by and stood beside the open desk next to me.

"Is this seat taken?" she asked.

"Be my guest." I put my hand out in welcome as my perma-grin sprang up instantly. What had started as kind of a sad Thursday got way better when Mme Depardieu announced a partnered exercise.

"Partners?" Rebecca asked me.

"*Oui!*" I said with way too much enthusiasm and flung my desk next to hers. I looked back at the girl I usually worked with, and she seemed okay with my sudden defection. In fact, she moved her desk next to the boy she liked. I laughed. Maybe changing partners would work out for both of us. *Ha! In my dreams,* I thought. What were the chances that Rebecca would ever notice me that way?

Mme Depardieu wanted us to interview each other in French and then write down the responses. For homework, we were supposed to write an essay in French about our partner.

Rebecca asked me the first question on the worksheet. "*Quel pays aimerais-tu visiter le plus et pourquoi?*"

Her soft brown eyes waited for my answer as her pen hovered over her worksheet. How could I think with her staring at me? I guess I was supposed to answer France or something, but I said, "England. Wales, I mean."

Mme Depardieu must have had supersonic hearing because she yelled at me, "*En français seulement*, Devon."

In the light of Rebecca's eyes, I had forgotten the French-only rule. How could I explain to my teacher that I couldn't think because Rebecca made my insides jittery? That she smelled so good, like roses, which fogged up my brain big time?

"*Pourquoi l'Angleterre? Le Pays de Galles?*" Rebecca asked as if she didn't notice my complete meltdown.

"Oh, uh, *je suis en partie galloise.*" I hoped Mme Depardieu wouldn't yell at me again for my "Oh, uh," but I didn't know how to say those words in

34

French.

"I didn't know you were part Welch," Rebecca whispered in English. "My family is mostly from the Islands. My mother's mother was from Jamaica. *J'aimerais vraiment y aller un jour.*" She must have remembered to speak French at the last minute, but then she whispered, "And now you don't have to ask me that question, do you?"

I laughed and wrote down Jamaica on my own worksheet.

She read the second question from the sheet. "*À quelle fac veux-tu aller?*"

What university? That was an interesting question because only about sixty percent of the kids going to Grasse River High School actually went to college. But I planned to be part of that sixty percent, so I said, "Plattsburgh State." I didn't know how to say Plattsburgh State in French, so I used a French accent.

Rebecca laughed. "I want to go to NYU. *L'Université de New York.*"

"You do? I mean, *vraiment?*"

"They have an amazing dance program at NYU."

"You can major *en danse?*"

"*Bien sûr,*" she said as if everybody knew that. "I want to get *une licence* in Fine Arts." We had lapsed into a mixture of French and English—Frenglish, I guess—but I didn't care about the French-only rule because Mme Depardieu had unknowingly handed me a way to get to know Rebecca faster than smiles and waves across the noisy cafeteria.

"*C'est super, ça!* You're in the dance troupe here, right?"

"*Oui, mademoiselle* Devon. *Oui.* Are you coming to my concert?"

Of course, I would. Every single performance. "*Quand est-ce?*"

"In about a month. The week before *Noël.*"

"Cool." But even the thought of watching Rebecca dance on stage wasn't enough to stop the realization that this would be the first Christmas without Grandma. Rebecca and I had been leaning close together so Mme Depardieu wouldn't hear our Frenglish, but my sudden heartache made me sit back and pull away.

"Devon, what's wrong?"

"Christmas."

She seemed to understand because she grabbed my hand. A perverse side of me actually enjoyed having her console me in my pain, but then my pain overtook even that. As she held my one hand, I cried behind the other. Images of Christmases past came pouring into my mind. Grandma always gave Missy and me an extra fifty dollars, which we weren't supposed to tell our parents about. And we never did because it was our secret with Grandma. Grandma and I had lots of fun secrets. Like how she always wanted to be my partner on Sundays when we played bridge after dinner because she and I could cheat really well and not get caught. If I hadn't been so choked up, I might have laughed at the memory.

Rebecca's hand rubbed my back while she murmured in French, "*Oui, je sais, c'est difficile! Courage*, Devon, *courage*."

Listening to her whisper sympathy to me in French brought me back to the present. I did that breathing thing she taught me and got myself under better control.

"That's it," she encouraged. "You're okay, now." She rubbed my back and squeezed my hand one last time.

"*Merci.*" I cleared my throat, and even though I didn't want to, I said, "I think we'd better do our worksheets."

"Only if you're okay."

I looked into her deep brown eyes. "I'm okay with you here." Something softened in her eyes, and I would have gotten lost in them if the other students weren't in the room. She continued to hold my gaze but then looked down at her desk.

I overstepped. I scared her. Oh my God, I got too pushy. What an idiot.

I felt the tension spread around us like an early-morning fog, but we managed to finish the worksheets just as the bell rang. Rebecca stood up and said, "Jessie said okay to a basketball interview. Do you still want to do it?"

Not really, I thought, *but if I can be closer to you, then yeah, I want to do it.* "Okay, sure." My inner voice screamed at me to run as far away from Jessie as possible.

"How's lunch tomorrow?"

"Cool." It was a date but with the wrong girl.

~~~

I studied the list of questions for my interview with Jessie as I ate Gail's tuna fish sandwich and she ate my turkey sandwich. She and Joey sat as close together as two people reasonably could, although I think she would have been in his lap if she could have gotten away with it.

Gail leaned toward me. "So, which one are you interviewing?"

"Oh, Jessie Crowler." I pointed to Jessie's back, four tables away. "She's the captain of the girls' basketball team."

"Senior?"

"Yeah." I took the last bite of her sandwich. "Good sandwich today."

"Well, amazing things happen when I make lunch."

Jessie turned around and looked toward me and Gail. I caught a quick glimpse of Rebecca pointing at me and saying something to Jessie. When Rebecca noticed me looking, she smiled and waved. I waved back and tried not to let my perma-grin take over my face.

Jessie and Rebecca stood up from their table and headed my way. I shoved Gail's plastic sandwich bag and my used napkin into the paper lunch bag and stood up to meet them. I hadn't eaten my little bag of carrots yet, so I shoved them into the pocket of my jeans. I'd eat them later.

Gail leaned toward me and said, "She looks like a guy."

"Who?"

"Jessie. Look at her." She leaned closer and whispered, "She's probably a lezzie."

Gail's words were an invisible slap. I got up and said tersely, "I'll be back later."

"Okay, later," Gail said, oblivious to my coldness. She simply went back to hanging all over Joey.

I rolled my eyes behind Gail because she completely missed my subtle departure. Gail and I used to talk to each other every day on the phone, but now that she had Joey, we only talked once in a while, and she usually ended our calls with something like, "Oh, I've got another call. It's Joey." or "Joey's picking me up, so I have to get ready." At first, that kind of hurt my feelings, but I got used to it. I mean, I had no choice. And now, on top of that, I didn't know if my best friend could accept me for who I was.

I met Jessie and Rebecca in the aisle. "Hey," I said to Rebecca and nodded to Jessie.

Rebecca introduced us. "Devon, this is Jessie. Jessie, Devon."

Jessie stuck out her hand, so I reached and shook it. Jessie had the look of an athlete. She wore tight, faded jeans and a white long-sleeved t-shirt. The t-shirt did nothing to hide her strong, muscular body. The gold chain around her neck held a colorful pendant in the shape of Africa. The red, green, and yellow stood out against her white shirt. Gail was wrong. Jessie didn't look like a guy; she looked like a strong young woman. She looked like an accomplished athlete.

"Should we go outside?" I asked, trying to take charge as if I was. "This shouldn't take too long."

"Sure." Jessie led the way. She shoved the door open with so much force that I didn't know if she was trying to impress me or Rebecca.

Jessie sat down at the table under the overhang, closest to the door. Rebecca sat next to her, and I grabbed a seat across from them. I couldn't tell if my hands shook from the cold or nerves.

Before any interview, I tell my subjects that anything said during the interview was fair game to be quoted. And if they didn't want to be quoted, they should say, "off the record," and I'd put my pen down or turn off the recorder.

Having given Jessie my disclaimer, I opened my notebook to the list of questions and said, "The team is supposed to do really well this year. What are your biggest challenges?"

I thought she might say something cocky, but to my relief, she thought about my question for a second and answered, "Well, Stone Lake always gives us trouble. We split with them last year, so we've learned never to take any team lightly. You know? On any given day."

She had such a tough exterior that her thoughtful and honest answer surprised me. Maybe I shouldn't have judged her so quickly. I mean, I didn't even know her.

"So," I continued, "there must be a lot of pressure on you in particular. Senior, captain."

"I guess so."

I don't think she expected this question, but I waited for her to elaborate. A good interviewer knows when to say nothing and let the subject keep talking.

And she did just that. "Everybody relies on me 'cuz I'm the point guard." She hesitated again, and I could sense the pressure she must have felt as the point guard. I hoped she'd elaborate because I had no idea in the world what a point guard did. "But once I get scoring, I'm pretty unstoppable."

Ah, there was the ego I knew she had. I just nodded and happily quoted her exact words. "Anything else?" I asked.

"Well, off the record—" She paused while I put my pen down. "There's pressure on me to represent." She struck a hip-hop pose with one hand on her chin.

"What do you mean?"

"Well, I'm Black, and I play basketball."

Again, I waited.

She continued. "It's such a cliché, you know? Like if you're Asian you're supposed to be good at math. And if you're Black, you're supposed to excel at hoops."

She was baiting me. I just knew it, but I didn't know what she wanted from me. Did she want me to make some kind of comment about her being Black? I decided not to say anything. When I didn't answer her, she just looked at Rebecca and said, "What are you gonna do? Right, babe?"

My mind screamed. *Babe? Did I hear that right?* Jessie just called Rebecca *babe*, and Rebecca just shrugged her shoulders.

"Hey, Becca," Jessie said, pulling a five-dollar bill out of her jeans pocket, "go get me a creamsicle."

"Now?"

"Yeah, now."

Rebecca hesitated for a second but then got up and left the table. She didn't even look at me, which made the uncomfortable silence between me and Jessie grow even more.

I cleared my throat and said, "I imagine, uh, all those things would create a lot of pressure on you." I swallowed hard. "Let's go back on the record." *Are you going out with Rebecca?*

As if to answer my question, Jessie snapped, "On the record, Raines." She poked the metal table with each word as her eyes burned a hole in my face. "Be careful, real careful around Rebecca."

I swallowed hard and managed to eke out, "What do you mean?"

Jessie stood up abruptly. "I'm warning you, Raines. Don't play with fire. Interview over." She stomped back across the gravel and slammed the cafeteria door open. It was only when the door shut again I realized that I'd been holding my breath.

Chapter 5

The Mall

For the next five days—over the weekend and all day Monday and Tuesday—I brainstormed how to get Rebecca to tell me why Jessie hated me. I couldn't talk about it with Gail or even with Missy. I just wanted to know what the heck Jessie thought I did to her, especially when I hardly knew her. Maybe Jessie could read minds. If so, then I was in big trouble.

On the way to Wednesday's French class, it dawned on me that maybe I had unintentionally broadcast my crush on Rebecca or something. I thought I had been careful. But then, speaking about careful, Jessie called Rebecca *babe*. Maybe they were together. Maybe I should come out to Rebecca. But then again, maybe I shouldn't because I had no idea if Rebecca and Jessie were together. Maybe they were just two friends who called each other *babe*. Part of me—well, most of me, actually—didn't buy the "just friends" things. Gail and I had been close friends since fourth grade, and we didn't call each other *babe*. More like dork or nimrod or gray-matter-challenged. But not *babe*. Jessie slipped. Or maybe it wasn't a slip. Maybe she wanted me to know they were girlfriends and that Rebecca was off-limits.

It was all really confusing, and I couldn't make sense of any of it. I simply shook my head as I walked up the steps to French. I needed to get out of my head. My troubles were small compared to everybody else's in the free world. It was Veteran's Day, and with so many kids joining the military right out of Grasse River High School, it was one of the town's biggest holidays. We'd even had a moment of silence during homeroom for some former students who were recently killed in the war. The announcement kind of bummed everybody out, and it made me wish I could have gone to the parade that morning. Maybe Rebecca would have wanted to go, too, but since the parade kicked off at 11:00

in the morning, we were stuck at school. My dad told me they always had the parade on November 11 at 11:00 because they signed the treaty ending World War I on that date and time. Rebecca and I would have had to cut school to go to the parade anyway, but I didn't think Rebecca was into cutting school. And, besides, Rebecca probably wasn't into hanging out with me, so what was I thinking anyway?

I got settled in my usual seat and looked up so I could watch her walk in. She smiled and made her way to the back of the room. I tried to hide my excitement over her apparent permanent change in seats.

"*Bonjour*, Ms. Journalist. *Comment va le journal?*"

"*Bonjour,* Ms. Dancer. The newspaper's fine. Being an editor ain't easy, though. Some of these people can't place a comma if their lives depended on it."

When she laughed, the sweet sound yanked my perma-grin out from the depths where I had stuffed it. I could dedicate my life to making her laugh.

"That must be a tough job," she said. "Just promise me one thing."

Anything. Everything. "What?"

"If I ever misplace a comma, be gentle. Okay?"

I burst out laughing. Several other kids turned our way, but I didn't care. I smiled at her and knew the smile took over my whole face. "I will always be gentle with you." *Whoa, did I just say that?* I hadn't meant to flirt. It just came out.

Rebecca seemed to take my flirting in stride, though. She said, "*Toi, oui,* Devon Raines, I'm sure you would."

Mme Depardieu called the class to order. We were going to read some kind of short story in the textbook, all in French, of course, and then answer questions on a worksheet.

As Mme Depardieu handed out the worksheets, Rebecca leaned over and whispered, "I got my application."

"What application?"

"The Karen Swanson School of Dance in New York. It's a summer program."

"Cool. When will you find out?"

"Well, I just got the application yesterday, but I have to send it back right away. If they like how I look on paper, Ms. Adams says they'll ask for an audition video. She told me if they ask for that, it usually means you'll get in."

"That's so cool. I hope they ask for your video." I reached for my worksheet from the girl in front of me.

"Me, too."

We read in silence for a while and answered the questions on the worksheet. I didn't know all the words in the story, but I was pretty good at winging it. I hoped I could wing it with Rebecca because I had no idea how to find out if she was into girls the same way I was. Maybe Missy would know how you told somebody that you liked them.

Mme Depardieu collected the worksheet with about five minutes left in the period. The way she tossed them into her "papers to be graded" basket told me we wouldn't be getting them back anytime soon. When she sat at her desk and started typing on her keyboard, the class knew that the lesson was over for the day.

"That was fun," I said to Rebecca sarcastically.

"Yeah, a real blast." She rolled her eyes. "Actually, speaking of fun, we're going to the mall on Saturday. Do you want to go?"

I never realized how such a simple question could turn me inside out. *Yes, yes, yes,* I screamed inside my head. **Omigod, Omigod, Omigod.** I didn't even care who the "we" referred to.

"Sure," I said with as much cool and calm as I could muster, with my heart beating a thousand miles an hour. I tried to ask her what time, but the question got caught in my throat. I coughed and tried again, "What time?"

"Oh, I don't know. We've got a couple of days to decide that, but Jessie usually likes to eat at the food court, and Natalie, well, she doesn't care when we go."

Jessie. Bummer. Of course, the "we" would include her. She wouldn't do anything to me with Rebecca right there. Would she?

"Okay," I said, "let me know on Friday." Most of me knew I shouldn't go to the mall with them, but the prospect of hanging out with Rebecca made the stupid part of me take over.

"Great." She reached down into the front pocket of her backpack and pulled out her cell phone. Keeping it low under her desk, she asked me for my cell number. My insides started shaking as she punched the numbers in. She saved it and said she'd text me later with the details. She snuck her cell phone back into her backpack and then looked up at me with mischief in her eyes as if we had just gotten away with something grand in Mme Depardieu's class.

The bell rang to end the period, and Rebecca bolted up and out of her seat. I got up to walk out with her, but when I saw Jessie waiting in the hallway, I looked down because I didn't want to see the daggers Jessie would shoot at me. I sat back down, defeated. Oh well, I thought to myself, in order to hang out with Rebecca, I'd have to hang out with Jessie, too. I'd better get some thicker armor. I guess I didn't wait long enough because when I looked up again, Jessie shot a couple of daggers my way from the open doorway. I swallowed hard around the sudden lump in my throat.

~~~

As we strolled through the food court at the Maplewoods Mall that Saturday, Natalie and I walked a step behind Jessie and Rebecca. They picked me up at my house around 11:30, and by 12:15, we were in the food court trying to figure out what to eat. Jessie and Natalie went for Chinese, but I decided on a turkey wrap with sprouts and cucumbers. Rebecca, seeming torn, opted to go with me to the wrap place. Ha! Devon 1, Jessie 0. I knew that was childish, especially since Jessie hadn't sent me a single dirty look all day, but still, it felt good for a moment.

When we regrouped at a table near the Chinese food counter, Jessie shoved a big spoonful of fried rice into her mouth, and with her mouth full, she said, "Hey, we can't always eat fried chicken and watermelon. Right, Devon?"

'Fried chicken and watermelon?' What did that mean?

Rebecca threw Jessie an exasperated look—one that said, "Behave." That's when I understood. Fried chicken and watermelon were supposed to be *Black* foods or whatever. And I was white. I was a white girl sitting at a table with three Black girls. Maybe this was why Jessie hated me. 'Cuz I was white. But that didn't make any sense. She had white friends. I think. I mean, most of her teammates were white. I never thought of myself as prejudiced, but maybe I was. I mean, I'd never hung out with any of the Black kids before. I decided to stay mute and not go for the bait.

When Rebecca smiled at me in apology, I felt better. She did this, of course, when Jessie wasn't looking. I smiled back and shrugged as if to say, "I'm not sure what I did to provoke that." I think I scored another point with her.

After lunch, we walked the mall. Early November seemed way too soon for Christmas stuff, but all the stores were decorated for the December holiday. We passed an electronics store with some of those mechanical puppies out front that barked and did flips. They were cute, but we didn't stop to look, even though I kind of wanted to.

Even though I had gained a few points at the food court, they didn't seem to matter since Natalie and I were relegated to second-class status again behind Jessie and Rebecca. We'd tried to walk four across, but the sea of people forced us to walk two and two. A lot of Canadians had come across the Seaway International Bridge to shop in the United States. I didn't really mind walking with Natalie because she loved to talk about basketball, and I was learning a lot about the sport. She was a sophomore, a little overweight, but not to the point of obesity or anything. She was just a big girl. She wore her hair down, like Rebecca, but Natalie's hair was shorter, coming just to her collar.

"So, what exactly does a power forward do?" I asked her.

"Oh, uh, I'm kind of a cross between a center and a regular forward."

I laughed. "Okay, that's as clear as mud."

Jessie must have been listening because she said over her shoulder, "Her job is to rebound the ball and then find me so I can dribble up the court, make a behind-the-back move around the defense, and lay it up as soft as a baby's behind."

I only understood about half of what she said. "Oh," I said as if impressed with Jessie's skills. I refused to antagonize her, even though she clearly had a problem with me.

Rebecca decided she wanted to look at earrings in one of those free-standing carts in the middle of the walkway. I think she was trying to change the subject, and for that, I was grateful.

"Hey, Devon," Rebecca said and beckoned me over. She held up a pair of small hoop earrings. "I think you'd look great in these." She held the earrings up to my ears as I looked in the mirror on the cart. I tried to focus on the earrings, but Rebecca's smile reflected in the mirror overtook me. I tried to keep my sanity with her standing so close, but her rose-scented perfume wrapped itself around me, making it hard to think straight.

I dug out the ten-dollar bill I had in my jeans pocket to pay for the $6.99 pair of earrings. I usually didn't spend money on jewelry, mainly because I get some at Christmas or birthdays from Mom, Missy, or Grandma. In fact, my grandmother gave me the pair of gold ball earrings I usually wear. I felt the now-familiar clench of my stomach when I thought of her. I forced it away. There was no way I was going to cry in front of Jessie. No way.

Rebecca seemed pleased when I took them to the cashier at the far end of the cart and stood with me while I paid. Jessie and Natalie stood together in the walkway where we'd left them. They didn't even pretend to be interested in the jewelry. Instead, they made fun of people walking by, including a really fat lady who walked by them. Without saying a word, Jessie waddled after her. That cracked up Natalie, who in turn waddled in a circle. I pretended to be oblivious to them, but out of the corner of my eye, I could see the serious look on Rebecca's face.

Change and bag in hand, I turned toward Rebecca and said, "Ready?" My heart leaped when I saw the troubled look in her eyes. Her cheeks were flushed, and I could tell that Jessie had embarrassed her. Thank God the fat lady didn't notice them making fun of her.

"C'mon." Rebecca put a hand on my back and nudged me toward her friends.

We resumed our original pecking order as we walked the full length of the mall. When we hit the Sears at the end, we turned back around and walked up the other side. Natalie continued to talk about basketball and the Connecticut Sun, her favorite WNBA basketball team. I'd pretty much had my fill of basketball by that point, but I asked her questions anyway just to keep the conversation going. What I really wanted to do was vaporize Jessie so I could walk next to Rebecca. I'd take her hand, and we wouldn't even care if people stared at us—two girls holding hands in the mall. But unfortunately, Jessie still existed. And although, technically, I was spending the afternoon with Rebecca,

I just wanted to go home at that point. Editing bad copy on a Saturday afternoon was beginning to sound much more appealing than playing second fiddle to Jessie.

As we walked back up the other side of the long stretch of the mall, an interracial couple walked toward us. A tall Black man held hands with a noticeably pregnant white woman. Once we passed them, Jessie shook her head and said, "They're dilutin' the blood, man." She turned toward Rebecca and said, "Don't they see that?"

Rebecca just glared at Jessie.

Jessie shrugged and said, "What? I was just kidding."

I didn't think she was kidding, though, and I realized that all day I'd felt aware and self-conscious about the color of my skin. Did Rebecca feel that kind of thing, too? I had no idea how to ask or even if I should.

~~~

I sat in my room after they dropped me off from the mall and tried to edit the girls' soccer article, but my mind kept wandering back to that afternoon. I liked stealing smiles from Rebecca, but overall, I didn't have much fun. I was hoping Rebecca would text me or something, but so far nothing.

I tried one last time to focus on the soccer article, but I closed the file in frustration and shut down the computer. I got up and took my new earrings out of their small plastic bag, then took off my gold ball earrings. I lifted the lid to my jewelry box and laughed. I'd have to ask Mom for a grown-up jewelry box for Christmas this year. The cheesy Howe Caverns stamp on the top of my current one reminded me of our family car trip we took to the Finger Lakes in the summer when I was ten. Grandma and Grandpa came with us on that trip, too. I didn't even choke up at the memory. Maybe I was making progress.

I carefully put on my new hoops. They were only about a half inch in diameter, but still, I'd never worn any kind of hoops before. I felt more grown up all of a sudden. I'd definitely have to wear them to school on Monday. Especially if I put my hair up. With my new earrings and new highlights, maybe Rebecca would look at me the way I wanted her to, not just as a friend, but maybe something more.

I sighed and gently placed the earrings Grandma had given me in the cedar box and then shut the lid. There was no way I could have ever told Grandma about me. About liking girls, that is. She had been kind of old-fashioned, but maybe she knew now. Maybe she looked down from heaven and was okay with me. And Grandpa, too. Maybe they'd know that being a lesbian wasn't a choice or something I just decided to be. Maybe they would understand that I wasn't some evil, horrible person and that it was just something I figured out about myself in seventh grade. My crush on Marcy Berger didn't last long, but the deep attraction I had for her back then woke up something inside me. When Missy wasn't around, I secretly searched the Internet for anything gay-related and discovered a whole world of gay people. They called it "the gay and lesbian community" on a few websites. I didn't know if Grasse River had one of those communities, but I hoped someday I'd find it if there was one. And those websites were right. I wasn't a lesbian because I chose to be. I just was. So there.

I don't know how I got there, but I found myself in Grandma's room. I took a deep breath. I hadn't gone into her room since she died. Nothing had been touched. Well, except for a couple of things. Mom had washed the sheets and comforter and remade the bed. She had been taking the sheets off the bed when I was trying to figure out what to wear to the mall. I sat on the edge of Grandma's newly made bed. Who would sleep in this bed next? Probably Missy. Eventually, she'd take her room back.

I smoothed out the comforter with my hand. The softness reminded me of times I'd sit on her bed, and we'd talk about stuff. Stuff like the animal shelter, her bridge club, or my school. I choked up a little, so I stood up and went to Grandma's bookshelf. Darn, Mom took the candy out of the jar, but that made sense because Grandma wasn't there anymore.

I picked up my favorite glass snow globe from Grandma's collection. I shook it and watched the snow swirl around the skyline of Manhattan. Missy brought this one back from New York when she went to a journalism conference last summer, and I'd probably go to that same conference when I went to Plattsburgh. Once all the snow settled on the bottom, I put the snow globe back and picked up a picture of Grandma and Grandpa standing in front of their Christmas tree. They looked young and confident, but there was a better word to describe them. Peaceful. I hoped they were at peace up in heaven.

I laughed at the picture of my dad and Uncle Joe as young boys. They looked so dorky in their old-fashioned clothes. Grandma even had an old elementary school picture of me and one of Missy. I hated my picture. Mom had gotten tired of brushing out the knots in my hair and had cut it way short into a page boy. The bangs were the biggest reason I hated the picture. Once I got into middle school, I informed my mother that I was going to grow out my hair. When she didn't protest at my first real rebellious act, it kind of knocked the wind out of my sails. After that, Missy helped me find a good style that I liked, one that framed my face nicely, as she put it. I hoped Rebecca liked my hair on Monday when I wore it up, though.

I put my school picture back on the dusty shelf and fled to my room. I didn't want my mom to see me crying in Grandma's room. I plopped on my bed and rolled into a fetal position. I smothered Grizzly tight to my chest and let myself cry for a while. I mostly cried about Grandma, but I think I also cried about the frustrating afternoon I'd spent with Rebecca and her friends. I made a promise to myself that I'd never be in a situation where I'd have to hang out with Jessie ever again. Of course, as soon as I made that promise, I knew that if Rebecca asked me to hang out with them all tomorrow, I'd do it. Who was I kidding?

I had to find out if Rebecca was like me. Was she into girls, too? But how did you find out something like that? It's not like I could come right out and ask her. Could I? And what if I did find out she was sapphically inclined? How did I tell her I liked her? How did I tell her that I loved French now because I got to see her every day? How did I tell her that what I felt for her was six thousand times more intense than what I'd ever felt for Marcy Berger? I had no idea.

~~~

A week after that stupid trip to the mall with Rebecca and Jessie, I waited in the backseat of Joey's car as he and Gail went into the P&C food store to get beer. Joey had his older brother's ID, and since they looked alike, most people didn't look at him twice. I think we were headed to Bruster Park to hang out with the regular Friday night crowd. Everybody went to Bruster on the weekends. Tonight, I'd hang there with Gail and Joey, and then tomorrow night, I'd head back there to hang out with Rebecca. Well, with Rebecca, Jessie, and Natalie. Even though I'd made that ridiculous vow never to go out in a group that included Jessie, I broke it.

Missy gave me some good advice when I called her last Sunday. I finally got the nerve to ask her about Rebecca. "Missy, how do you tell somebody you like them?"

"You mean *like* like?" Missy asked.

I could feel myself blush and was glad she couldn't see me over the phone. "Yeah."

"Okay," she said, "do you have any classes with them?"

"Yeah," I answered. "French."

Them. Again, Missy didn't say "him." I knew she was leaving it up to me to come out to her, but I just didn't know how. The only person I had ever come out to was myself, and even though I wanted desperately to tell my secret to at least one other person in the world, I didn't know if I could handle the rejection or hostility that I heard happened when people came out. I'd read horror stories on the Internet about people getting beaten up or thrown out of their houses. I'm sixteen; I didn't want to get thrown out of my house. Where was I supposed to go?

"Okay," Missy said, "do you sit near them? Because if not, maybe you should try to move your seat, if you can do that without making it too obvious, that is."

"Yeah, sh—" I stopped myself just in time. I had almost said, "she." Talking in code like this was tricky. "Actually," I tried again, "they moved their seat next to me last week."

"No kidding, squirt. I think you're already in. I think they already like you if they moved seats."

Missy had my attention now. "You think so? But what do I do now?"

"Well, have you invited them to hang out with you and Gail? You know, do something with a group of friends? That way, it won't seem like a date."

A date? The word scared me to death. "Um, I went out with some of her

50

friends to the mall last weekend." *Oh, shit, shit, shit. I just said, "her."* I held my breath, hoping Missy hadn't heard it.

And maybe she actually didn't hear my slip because she said, "Squirt, that's awesome. Just keep doing stuff like that, and if it's meant to be, then it'll happen."

"Yeah, okay."

"But don't push it. And you could always..."

"What? Always what?"

"You could always wait for them to make the first move, you know."

Oh, God. Maybe Rebecca already made the first move when she changed her seat. And maybe she made the second move by asking me to go to the mall. I rubbed my forehead when I realized she had probably already made the third move by asking me to go to Bruster with her. How many more hints did I need?

I guess I hadn't said anything while these thoughts sloshed through my brain because Missy said, "Hey, squirt, you still there?"

"Yeah, sorry. I'm just—" I took a breath and sighed it out in frustration. "I don't know. I'm new at this."

Missy laughed. "And it's the scariest thing, too. To like somebody and not know if they feel the same way."

Missy then started to tell me about a new guy she was seeing, but she used definite pronouns this time. "*His* name is Brandon. *He's* studying chemistry. *He's* a junior, too."

Joey and Gail came back to the car, knocking me out of my thoughts. Joey lifted the grocery bag. "We scored," he said triumphantly. He put the brown grocery bag filled with what looked like two six-packs of beer on the seat next to me.

"Cool," I said. I hated beer, actually, but everybody went to Bruster to drink beer, so that's what we were going to do, too.

From the passenger seat, Gail said, "Yeah, the cashier hardly even looked at Joey. She just took the ID and glanced at it." She gazed at Joey with such admiration that once again, I felt like a voyeur, a spy, a fifth wheel. And when Joey got in, closed the driver's side door, and looked back at Gail the same way, I decided that, yeah, I was intruding. Gail only asked me to tag along because she felt guilty about spending so much time with Joey and not with me.

"Hey, guys," I called from the backseat. "You know what? I don't feel so hot all of a sudden. Maybe I should go home."

"Oh, Devon," Gail said, turning full around to look at me. "Are you sure? Do you want us to go back in and get you something? Aspirin?"

I laughed. "No, I'll be okay. I just need to go home, I think." I didn't like lying to her, but I would have been uncomfortable hanging out in the backseat, knowing they just wanted to be alone together.

"Okay," Gail said. "If you're sure. We'll try again another time."

Joey drove the couple of miles back to my house and dropped me off. Before he pulled out, I watched Gail lean over and give him a long kiss. Yup, I definitely read the signs right. Was I reading Rebecca's signs right?

Chapter 6

Stranded

I brushed my hair in front of the bathroom mirror, debating whether to wear it up or down. Down, I decided. Rebecca wouldn't see much of me in Jessie's dark car anyway, so why bother? Rebecca's eyes lit up on Monday when she saw me wearing my new hoop earrings. So, I definitely had to wear them again tonight.

I looked at myself for an extra second in the mirror. Grandma always said I was pretty. I wasn't so sure, but at least I had a good nose—kind of straight, but not too big and not too small. Okay, so maybe I had one good feature, but you couldn't just walk around telling people to only look at your nose; that would be weird. Did Rebecca like my nose?

Gail called earlier in the day and told me she was sorry I had to go home the night before. I think she kind of missed the closeness we used to have. I know I did. I missed hanging out with her, but I guess things were changing for both of us. When she asked me what I was doing that evening, I lied. I don't know why I lied, but I told her I was going to stay home and work on newspaper stuff. For some reason, I didn't want to tell her that I was going to hang out at Bruster with Rebecca. Well, Rebecca and her friends, that is.

I wanted to tell Gail I was a lesbian, but I didn't know how. Maybe after she got over the initial shock, she could give me advice about Rebecca, but then again, I'd probably tell Missy first and see how that went. I wasn't sure now if Rebecca's *signs* were signs at all, and I didn't want to end up looking like an idiot.

I put the hairbrush down and stood back. So far, so good, but now I only had a half hour before they came to pick me up, and I still had to figure out what to wear. I wish we didn't have to hang outside in November, but we had nowhere else to go. We'd already done the mall thing, so Bruster was next, I guess.

I went into my room and pulled out a pair of black jeans, my black cowboy boots that pinched my toes, and a green turtleneck sweater. Actually, the sweater was Missy's, but she hadn't taken it to Plattsburgh, so I figured she wouldn't mind if I borrowed it this once.

I scurried out of my robe and dressed in record time. Dad was on a thermostat kick again, so the house was arctic. I couldn't risk frostbite before my date with Rebecca, or I'd never know if she liked me. I scolded myself. This wasn't a date. This was just hanging out with some new friends from school.

I checked myself one last time in the mirror and put my wallet in my back pocket. I didn't think I'd need money, but I had ten bucks—next week's lunch money. I was heading out my bedroom door when I noticed my robe on the floor. I turned on my heels, picked up the robe, and hung it in the closet, which was weird because I usually just left my clothes on the floor, and then Missy or Mom would yell at me. But for some reason, I felt like picking it up. I guess I was thinking that Rebecca probably would have picked up her robe, so I should, too.

I made one quick stop in Grandma's room and picked up my favorite snow globe. I shook it hard, and as I watched the snow settle over the Empire State Building, I said, "Grandma, wish me luck tonight. I want Rebecca to give me a sign." I sighed and put the snow globe back. I made a quick promise to Grandma to come back to her room one of these days and dust her shelves.

I practically skipped out of Grandma's room, down the hall, and down the steps. I looked out the window by the front door and breathed a sigh of relief. They weren't here yet.

I jumped when my mom spoke.

"Are your new friends here?"

"You scared me, Mom." I sat on the couch next to her armchair. "No, they're not here. Rebecca said they'd be here at seven."

"Now, who are these girls again?" She took her reading glasses off and put down her book.

"I told you. Rebecca is Mr. Washington's daughter. You know—the funeral director?" I kind of whispered the last out of respect. I didn't want to remind my mom about our recent sadness. "And a couple of her friends, too."

"Okay," she said, picking up her book. "With your dad working overtime, please don't stay out too late because I don't want to have to worry about both of you."

"I won't." I heard a car horn blare from the driveway, and my heart thumped into my throat. "Oh, that's them," I squeaked and hoped Mom didn't pick up on my excitement.

I grabbed my hooded sweatshirt out of the closet, threw it on, and then put my jean jacket on over that. I yanked open the front door and was about to bolt outside when my mom said, "Do you have your keys?"

I smacked the front pocket of my jeans. "Yup."

"Cell phone?"

I reached into the inner pocket of my jean jacket and felt the familiar rectangular shape. "Yup."

"Do you need money?"

"Nope." I smiled at my mom and said, "But thanks. I'll see you later."

I bolted out the front door before she could ask me any more questions, and I slammed the door harder than I meant to. I heard her call, "Have a good time."

Oh, I would. Or at least I hoped I would.

Jessie's dark blue four-door—a Ford Focus, I think—idled in the driveway. I melted when I saw Rebecca's bright smile from the front passenger seat. She had her hair pulled back into a ponytail, but then she had it flipped up with a barrette to keep it off her neck. I opened the back door behind Rebecca, and as I got in, Natalie slid over behind Jessie. I shut the door quickly to keep out the cold.

Rebecca turned all the way around to face me. "Hey, Devon."

"Hey." I smiled back at her, but then I let my smile include Jessie and Natalie, too. "Thanks for picking me up."

"It's cool," Jessie said and put the car in reverse. She backed the car out of the driveway and then headed down my street in the direction of Bruster Park.

I wasn't sure what was going to happen that night, but I found out soon enough it involved some kind of light beer from Milwaukee because Jessie handed me a bottle from the front seat, and Natalie handed me an opener.

"Oh, okay. Thanks." I took both the beer and the opener. I wasn't a beer drinker, but I was hanging out with Rebecca and her friends, and whatever they did, I'd do.

Jessie looked at me for a second and said, "Just keep it down so the cops won't see."

"Okay." I popped the top and took a sip. Nope, I still didn't like the taste. I'd probably nurse this one all night if I could get away with it.

The car got kind of quiet at that point, and I sensed that maybe they weren't sure what to talk to me about. I cleared my throat and asked, "So, you guys had a game today, right?"

"Scrimmage," Jessie said as if I should know the difference between a game and a scrimmage. Which, honestly, I should have known since I was now a sports editor.

"Okay," I admitted. "What's the difference?"

"A scrimmage doesn't really count," Natalie said. "Coach just tries out all kinds of lineups and plays to see what works best. But," she clapped Jessie on the shoulder, "we beat Riverton!"

Jessie punched the air with her beer as she drove. "That's right! Get used to it."

"We're unstoppable," Natalie added.

I decided to stay on the basketball topic. "Your first real game is Friday?"

"Yeah." Jessie took a swig of beer. "The day after Thanksgiving."

"I'll have to come by and check it out." I probably said it with too much enthusiasm, but I was trying to make peace with Jessie even though I wasn't sure what I'd done for her to hate me.

Rebecca turned to face me. "They're playing in the Grasse River Turkey Tournament. The finals are Saturday, and we're supposed to win the whole thing."

"S'right," Jessie said and saluted Rebecca with her beer. So much for keeping the beer out of sight from the cops.

"A tournament?" I asked. "How many teams?"

"Just four," Natalie said. "Us included. It's a pre-season double-elimination tourney, and we play teams we won't ever see again. These games will count in our overall standings, though, but not in the St. Lawrence League.

56

But we should be at least three and oh, on Saturday."

"Damn straight." Another beer salute from Jessie. That rule about keeping the beer out of sight must have been for everybody else.

I felt kind of stupid because I knew next to nothing about sports, so I decided that I needed to become a major fan of every girls' sport at school. I didn't want Mrs. Gibson to think she'd made a mistake promoting me to editor, so I decided that I should go to as many games as I could. And I'd start with Friday's girls' basketball game. And, oh yeah, as a bonus, Rebecca would be there.

The tires crunched the gravel as Jessie pulled into Bruster Park. She found an empty parking spot near the softball backstop. In the summer, a lot of softball leagues play in the park. I remember one time last summer when Mom, Dad, and I drove past the field, and even though it only took us about fifteen seconds to go by, I saw a whole bunch of women in softball t-shirts who might be like me. Some had short hair and didn't look like moms or housewives or anything. That was a Tuesday night, and I remember desperately wanting to go back and see those women, even though I wasn't into softball all that much. But I never could figure out how to get back to the field without raising suspicion. I didn't have my driver's license—I wouldn't get that until my birthday in February—so I couldn't just borrow the car. And I couldn't ask my mom to drop me off. What was I going to say? "Mom, I want to go to Bruster Park on Tuesday night so I can check out some girls." Yeah, right. I guess I could have asked Missy to drop me off, but I wasn't ready to come out to her then, either. Or maybe I could have just gone for a jog, but Bruster's about five miles away from home, and a ten-mile round-trip run wasn't that appealing. The biggest thing stopping me, though, was that I didn't know what I would do once I got there. I mean, I wouldn't know anybody, and there was no way I'd ever get up enough nerve to talk to anybody.

I heard myself sigh as if from another life. I hoped nobody heard me because I didn't want them to think I was nervous or anything.

Jessie turned off the engine, and the heater went off. Even though the car was still nice and warm, the cold would seep in pretty quickly.

"Hey, Devon." Jessie leaned back against the driver's side door and turned her head to face me.

"Yeah?"

"How's that beer going down?"

I had forgotten about it, actually. "Oh, good." I tipped the bottle and took a sip.

Natalie leaned her beer toward mine. "Cheers," she said and took another sip. She then clinked her bottle against mine.

"*Tchine!*" I said back.

"*À ta santé, aussi*," Rebecca said to Natalie and me in the backseat. She tipped her bottle in salute.

I laughed. "*Toi aussi, à ta santé*," I said back at her.

"Oh, don't start that French shit," Jessie said. "You know I don't understand it."

"Me, neither," Natalie added.

"*Excuse-moi*," Rebecca said in French, but then laughed.

"Yeah, we're sorry." I suppressed a grin.

"Whatever," Jessie said, sounding dismissive. "I asked you how you liked your beer because everybody has to chip in."

I immediately felt like an idiot because I hadn't offered to give them any money. "Oh, I'm sorry. Of course, I'll chip in. How much?" I reached into my back pocket, knowing I only had the ten. Hopefully, she'd have some change.

"Ten," Jessie said with a definite challenge in her voice.

"Ten? For what?" I blurted before I could stop my mouth from engaging. That was my lunch money for the next two school days. "I don't think—"

"You special or something?" Jessie interrupted snidely. "We all pitched in ten bucks. You don't think you have to put in the same?"

"Here," I said and handed her the last of my money. What I'd been going to say was that I didn't think I'd have more than one beer, but I decided two things right then. One—I'd enjoy my ten-dollar beer so that I wouldn't appear confrontational in front of Rebecca, and two—this was the absolute last time I would hang out with Jessie in any situation. Even if it meant I couldn't hang out with Rebecca anymore.

Jessie put my money in her pocket. "Everybody's equal here," she said in a matter-of-fact tone. I think she was trying to tell me that everything was going to work out between us as long as I understood that she was in charge.

I tried to keep my voice even as I responded, "Hey, no problem. I should have offered to pay my share right away." *Which was probably about fifty cents, not ten freakin' bucks*, I shouted in my head.

Jessie saluted me with her beer and then drained it. She handed the empty bottle to Natalie, who put it in a P&C grocery bag on the seat. Jessie popped open a fresh one and held it out toward me. "Ready for another?"

"No, I'm good."

Natalie put her empty bottle in the bag, and Jessie handed her a full bottle.

Rebecca turned to me and asked, "So, how's the newspaper going?"

Thank God somebody changed the subject. At least I had one ally in the car. "Great," I said. "The field hockey team is still undefeated, and they'll probably make it to states."

"Just like we will." Jessie clinked bottles with Natalie.

"Oh, yeah," Natalie agreed. She turned to me and asked, "Do you write all the stories?"

"Oh, God, no. I'm just the editor. I mean, I might write one or two, but I check all the articles for grammar, length, and content. But actually, I'll be the one writing the winter sports previews, including your basketball team." And what I didn't say out loud was, "And so you should treat me better. Don't cha think?"

Rebecca said, "Sounds like a lot of work." She gulped down the last swig of beer and handed her empty bottle to Natalie. Jessie didn't hesitate and popped open another one for her. Rebecca smiled at Jessie and said, "Thanks," which stabbed me right in the heart. I didn't want Rebecca to smile at Jessie that way. Only me.

We spent the next hour or so talking about school and college plans. I got the distinct feeling that Natalie was Jessie's number one fan because she agreed with everything Jessie said and was a master at stroking Jessie's already over-inflated ego.

Jessie started up the car and put the heater back on. Thank God because my hands were starting to become icicles. I almost wished I'd worn a scarf and brought gloves, but no way was I going to look like a dork in front of Jessie.

I was amazed at how many beers Jessie, Natalie, and even Rebecca drank. I still had the first one Jessie gave me over an hour ago. Although I had managed to choke down about three-quarters of it, each swallow was a struggle.

Jessie was in the middle of her nineteenth story about her basketball prowess when Rebecca announced, "I have to go to the bathroom."

Jessie seemed annoyed at having her story interrupted and gestured toward the woods with her beer, which caused some of it to splatter on the dashboard. "You know where to go, Babe." The irritation in her voice was clear.

"Come with me?" Rebecca asked in a pleading voice.

"Nah. It's too cold, and I'm not done with my beer." Jessie turned up the car heater to full blast.

Rebecca turned to me with pleading eyes. I offered before I could stop myself. "I'll go with you."

"Okay," she said and opened her door.

I didn't dare look at Jessie when the interior light came on because I was afraid she'd flash me one of those evil looks or something. I flung open the back door and jumped out of the car. I held onto my beer so I could dump out the sour liquid somewhere in the woods.

Rebecca said to Jessie, "We'll be right back."

As she shut the passenger door, I heard Jessie bark, "Just hurry up."

I got white hot angry with Jessie at that moment. I couldn't believe how badly she treated Rebecca. If I were friends with Rebecca, I'd never yell at her or brag about how great I was or steal ten dollars from her friends. I'd throw rose petals at her feet and go wherever she wanted to go.

"This way." Rebecca beckoned and headed toward the stand of pine trees surrounding the softball field. "I hate coming out here in the dark by myself."

"Yeah," I said, falling in step with her, "it's kind of creepy out here." The way she picked her way down the trail made me think she'd done this before.

Rebecca said, "Thanks for coming with me."

"No problem. I needed to walk around, anyway." That was a big fat lie, but I had to say something, and I couldn't tell her that I just wanted to be alone with her.

"Thanks." She was about to say something else, but she stumbled on the pathway. "Whooey," she laughed. "Some graceful dancer I am. Too many

60

beers, I think."

"Are you okay?"

"Yeah. Hey, stop here. I'm going over..." She swayed as she pointed farther up the path to a dark stand of trees. "...there. Just give me one little second while I, you know."

"Okay." I turned away from her and moved behind some trees so Jessie couldn't see me from the car. I poured my flat beer out on one side of the path but put the bottle in my coat pocket. Once we got back in the car, I'd throw the empty bottle into the grocery bag.

After a couple of minutes, Rebecca made her way back. When I heard her behind me, I turned. Good thing I did because she stumbled again and fell into me. I caught her so she wouldn't fall.

"Whoops," she said as she leaned heavily against me. Her head came to rest against my shoulder, but her arms hung loosely by her sides as if she didn't want to go too far and actually hug me.

"Are you okay?" I put my arms around her waist so she wouldn't fall. I leaned my head back to try and see her face. Her eyes were closed, and she didn't say anything. My heart was pounding so hard I was sure she could hear it. "Rebecca?" I should have been ecstatic that I had her in my arms, but I was afraid she had passed out or something.

Her eyes fluttered open, and she picked her head up off my shoulder, but she didn't pull away. She flashed me that smile, the one that made me melt. She reached up and put the palm of her hand flat against my cheek. Her hand was cold, but it made me oh so warm. I couldn't decipher the look in her eyes, but the sadness in them was unmistakable.

She said, "*Tu es si belle,* Devon. *Si belle.*"

I almost forgot to breathe. She just told me I was beautiful. I swallowed hard and couldn't think of a single thing to say. Oh, but I wanted to kiss her. I think I would have if she hadn't pulled away.

"C'mon," she said. "Jessie's waiting." She walked up the path in front of me, but I couldn't get my feet to move. I was dizzy with confusion. What did it mean? I think, and I wasn't positive, but I think Rebecca had just given me that sign I wanted. I tried to hide my returning perma-grin because I couldn't get back in Jessie's car with this smile plastered on my face. She'd know in a second.

I finally got my feet moving, but I stopped at the edge of the trees and watched as Rebecca got in the car. I took a few deep breaths and made my way toward them, but before I even got to the lot, Jessie slammed the car into reverse and tore out of the parking spot.

"Wait! Jessie!" I yelled and ran toward the car, but as Jessie put the car in drive, she jabbed her finger at me and shook her head slowly as if to say there was no way I'd ever hang out with them again. She gunned the engine, causing gravel to fly everywhere as the car screamed out of the parking lot. I stood helpless as I watched the car disappear from view.

What just happened? Was this a joke? Rebecca wouldn't let Jessie leave me stranded in the cold. Would she? With that faith in mind, I walked back to the edge of the parking lot and sat on the guard rail to wait for my *friends* to come back. I don't know how long I waited, maybe twenty minutes, but I started to get seriously cold. Pacing around wasn't keeping me warm anymore. At this point, I was really pissed. How could Rebecca let Jessie leave me stranded like that? Or maybe, and I could barely bring myself to think it, maybe Rebecca had a part in it, too.

I bolted off the guard rail, feeling like an idiot, and started the five-mile trek home in tight boots, trying to figure out life and my role in it.

Chapter 7

Lonely

The very next morning, Rebecca texted me around 10:00, asking me to call her when I got a chance. I wanted to call her right away but decided to make her wait. Those five minutes were agony for me, but I finally relented and called her. She apologized over and over for leaving me. She said she didn't know Jessie had ditched me. Even with her attempts to smooth things over, I still had a heavy heart about what happened, but she continually reassured me she'd had no part in it.

She said she thought I was in the car when Jessie pulled out of Bruster. She told me she'd fallen asleep as the car left the park, claiming too much beer, and didn't even wake up when Jessie dropped off Natalie. She woke up later when Jessie pulled back into Bruster. She was confused when she discovered that Natalie and I were both gone. Jessie told Rebecca that Natalie and I said we were tired and wanted to go home, so she interrupted her evening and valiantly dropped us both off while Rebecca slept. *What a hero*. I scoffed silently as Rebecca told me this part of Jessie's farfetched tale.

When I asked Rebecca if she believed Jessie, she said, "I did at first. I mean, Jessie can be cold, but she's never been mean like that. But then she said something this morning. Something about you."

"What did she say?" I was afraid to hear what she'd said but kept in mind what Missy always told me—what a person does far outweighs what a person says.

"Well..." Rebecca seemed to hesitate as if she regretted bringing it up. "Jessie said she didn't know why we were hanging out with some white girl."

"Some *white* girl?" Did Rebecca see me this way, too? As just some white girl?

"I'm sorry, Devon. She can be kind of, I don't know, racist, I guess. And the mall last weekend—that was just a bad idea." Rebecca cleared her throat and added, "And then she said something about leaving the *white girl* to fend for herself. I badgered her until she confessed about ditching you at Bruster. I was so mad at her that I think she kind of felt bad about leaving you."

Just kind of? I thought sarcastically. I was going to tell her about having to walk five miles home in the dark. Talk about scary, but since Jessie was the one who abandoned me at the park, not Rebecca, I pretty much forgave her and said, "I'm just glad I could hang out with you last night." And even though she couldn't see me turning red, I hoped she knew I was giving her a sign.

I wasn't sure how to interpret her silence. "Rebecca?"

"Yeah?"

"Are you okay?"

She sighed into the phone and said, "Yeah," with such resignation in her voice that my heart lurched.

I wanted so badly to crawl through the cell phone tower and hug her. I wanted to make everything okay. I remembered looking out the window once I got home. I was looking toward Rebecca's house, totally defeated that she had abandoned me. I had no idea then what had happened. All I know is that I felt like the loneliest person in the world.

"Well, I'm just glad you're okay," Rebecca said. "I'm sorry about Jessie. She's just..."

"Just what?"

"Oh, I don't know. Possessive, I guess."

Possessive? They had to be going out. I was sure of it now.

Rebecca said she had to go, but I think she wanted to hang up because she was kind of embarrassed by what happened. I told her I'd see her at school the next day.

And now it was the next day, Monday afternoon to be precise, and I sat by myself in the cafeteria. That lonely feeling was back, but there wasn't much I could do about it, so I took the ham sandwich out of my lunch bag. For some strange reason, I didn't have any money for lunch, maybe because I had to pay ten bucks for a lousy beer on Saturday. I couldn't even trade with Gail because she and Joey snuck off school property to go to Subway. I said, "No, thanks," when Gail asked if I wanted to go with them. There were three reasons I didn't want to go. Mainly, I didn't want to get in trouble, but I also didn't want to intrude on their relationship. There was that third reason, of course. And it was the one that confused me the most. For some reason, even though Rebecca and her friends had ditched me at Bruster, I still wanted to see her—Rebecca, I mean.

I sat alone at the back table and tried to look comfortable by myself, like I was a lone wolf or something—secure and confident with my solitary status. I'm not so sure I was pulling it off, though. And to be honest, I felt like a loser. Maybe I was. I don't know. I snuck peeks at Rebecca now and then, but even though she was facing my direction, she never made eye contact with me. I was pretty sure she was avoiding me on purpose, even though I thought we had cleared up the misunderstanding about Bruster during our phone call. Maybe I was living in a delusional world. Yeah, that was probably it. I should move on, forget Rebecca existed, and stop playing the fool.

I looked down at my unread history book, which I'd opened so I wouldn't look like such a loser with no friends. I doubted my ruse was working. All I knew was that I felt as if everyone had abandoned me. Grandma died. Gail ditched me for Joey. And now Rebecca, even before we had a chance to become friends, had seemed nice, but now I wasn't so sure.

I mean, how could she be friends with a jerk like Jessie, anyway? Maybe she was like that, too. I snapped my baby carrot in half and almost laughed out loud at the violence of it. I could see the headline now. "Lone Wolf Tortures Carrot: Vegetarians Outraged." At least there was no one around to watch as I wallowed in self-pity.

~~~

I sat in the back of the French class, waffling between wanting Rebecca to sit in the back next to me and wanting her to go back to sitting in the front so I wouldn't have to interact with her. A lump jumped into my throat when she didn't hesitate and walked all the way to the back of the room. She plopped down next to me.

"Hey, Devon."

"Hey," I said back, noncommittally. I felt bad for some reason and threw out an olive branch by saying, "Did you finish the vocab?"

She didn't answer. She simply looked at me with an apology in her eyes.

Mme Depardieu started the class. "*Vocabulaire, s'il vous plaît.*"

I looked away from Rebecca and got out my French homework, wondering if we'd ever be friends.

Mme Depardieu called on students one at a time for definitions. I didn't want Mme Depardieu to think I was slacking off, so half of me actually paid attention to the vocabulary lesson while the other half went back to Bruster and wondered if Rebecca falling into my arms was the life-changing moment I hoped it was. Life-changing moments should be remembered. The warmth created by Rebecca's hand on my cheek was one of those moments. Wasn't it?

I focused more intently on the vocab as Mme Depardieu called on kids around me.

"Devon Raines. *Donnez une définition du mot 'cottage', s'il vous plaît.*"

Oh good, I thought, *an easy one.* "*Cottage* obviously means cottage or small house. My sentence would be—*Un jour, j'aimerais vivre dans un "cottage" au bord d'un lac, entouré par des pins, dans les Montagnes Adirondack.*"

"Zat sounds nice, Devon. My husband's family owned a cottage on Lake Meacham in zeh Adirondacks. *C'était merveilleux.* Okay, Rebecca Washington, please define *bateaux à rames.*"

"Okay," Rebecca said. "*Bateaux à rames* means rowboat. Um, let's see. Oh, okay, I've got one. *J'irais dans mon bateau à rames jusqu'au cottage de Devon qui donne sur le lac et je l'emmènerai pêcher.*"

"*Très bien*, Rebecca." Mme Depardieu laughed. "I'm sure Devon would love to go fishing wiz you in your rowboat." She laughed again and turned her back to the class to get something behind her desk.

I whipped my head around toward Rebecca. "Fishing? You?" I'd been fishing lots of times with my dad and grandpa, but it had been a while.

"I love fishing. And, yeah, I'll take you next summer if you want."

Of course, I wanted to go. 'The heart wants what the heart wants,' Missy sometimes said. And my heart wanted to do anything Rebecca did. My head followed along, making me silently vow to do anything if I could do it with her. Playfully, I asked, "Lures or worms?"

"Pfft," she said with mock disdain. "Worms, *bien sûr*. Fish want real food."

I nodded my head in agreement. Grandpa and Rebecca would have gotten along just fine. "Okay, you're on."

She stuck her hand out. "It's a date then."

I reached across the aisle and slid my hand slowly into hers. Her hand was warm this time. And soft. I held on longer than I should have and even held her gaze longer than I should have. She just smiled that sad smile I had seen too often lately and slowly pulled her hand from mine.

"Okay, ladies and gentlemen," Mme Depardieu directed. "Before you get to your reading, I wanted to tell you zat we are all set for our field trip to zeh St. Lawrence River and power dam tomorrow. The busses will be ready to board at 7:40 in front of zee school. Don't be late. We should be back for fifth period, but bring your lunches in case we get back late."

Mme Depardieu then instructed us to get out our textbooks and turn to a short story on page 120. A sketch of a cottage on a harbor in what looked like a fishing village took up about half the page. I guessed that the short story we were about to read would have all the vocabulary words we'd just gone over.

"*Continuez à lire en silence. Merci,*" Mme Depardieu said. And with those final instructions, she sat down at her computer and started typing.

Since we had to read to ourselves, I couldn't talk to Rebecca, but I just pretended to read the story. I could read it at home after the girls' sports banquet later. Right then, I had to use the time in class to come up with something to say to Rebecca in the ten seconds I'd have after the bell rang, and she bolted to meet Jessie at the classroom door.

Luckily, I'd see her all day during the field trip to the power dam tomorrow. That was a real plus. And Jessie wouldn't be there. Big double plus. And I was sure I'd see Rebecca again on Friday night at the basketball game. Maybe I could even sit with her. That would really grate Jessie's cheese for sure because she wouldn't be able to do a single thing about it.

But as I pretended to read, I still couldn't think of a single thing to say to Rebecca except maybe, "See you tomorrow," or "Save me a seat on the bus." I could write seventy million articles for the newspaper, but I couldn't think of a single thing to say to the gorgeous girl sitting next to me.

To distract myself, I thought about the preview piece I had to write about the girls' basketball team, but now, after the interesting developments at Bruster Park on Saturday, I figured the basketball preview would end up as a sideline. Yeah, and the rifle team would need at least a two-page spread with a full history of the sport, along with a full bio of each athlete. I hid an evil grin under my hand as I imagined the girls' basketball preview reduced to postage-stamp size, hidden away with the paid advertisements that nobody ever read. Of course, I'd never do anything like that. But scheming about it made me feel better.

I sighed, probably a little too loudly, because I felt Rebecca watching me. I looked over, and the smile in her eyes grew as we made eye contact. She wrote on the edge of a page in her notebook, "R U OK?" and turned it toward me so I could see.

I turned to a fresh page in my notebook and wrote, "Yes."

"Sorry about Saturday." She hesitated as if she wanted to write something else, but with a sigh, she pulled the pen away and turned the page toward me.

"Me, 2," I wrote. "I'm not mad @ U." Of course, that implied that I was mad at Jessie and even Natalie. I thought Natalie and I had been getting along great, but even Natalie hadn't stopped Jessie from leaving me at Bruster.

"U sure?" she wrote.

I decided then and there to wholeheartedly believe that Rebecca had been asleep and had no part in it. If I had kept even a sliver of doubt in my heart, then I'd never have been able to trust her. I wrote, "I'm sure." And I meant it.

She put her pen down, sat back, and mouthed the words, "Thank you." She looked so relieved that it made me feel good to make her feel better.

I mouthed back, "You're welcome."

She picked her pen back up and wrote, "Did I fall on U in the woods?"

Her question surprised me. I wasn't going to bring it up. "Yes." I couldn't think of anything to add, so I picked up my pen.

"Sorry. 2 much beer," she wrote in apology.

"That's okay."

"Clumsy," she wrote and pointed to herself.

I pointed again to what I had just written so she'd know that I really meant it. In fact, it was more than okay, but I didn't know how to tell her that. I wondered why she kept apologizing. But then, I had another epiphany. She had just asked me a bigger question, didn't she? Oh my God, she wanted to know how I felt about her falling into me, touching me on the cheek, and leaning on me way longer than necessary. That had to be her real question, so I answered honestly and wrote, "I'll catch you every single time," and pointed to myself. God, I hoped she really had meant for me to read between the lines.

~~~

My mom dropped me off at the Best Western hotel, but since the girls' sports banquet didn't start for another twenty minutes, I decided to call Missy from my cell phone. I walked to a remote area of the lobby and sat in one of those uncomfortable, overstuffed chairs. I faced the front door of the hotel so I could keep my eye on the people coming in. I was glad I was sitting with the soccer team so I could find out how they did in their last game and get their final record since the soccer article didn't have their final results.

I said, "Missy," into the phone, and it dialed my big sister in Plattsburgh. She picked up on the second ring. I knew she'd have her phone on her.

"Missy, it's me."

"Hey, squirt," she said. "You okay?"

"Yeah, I just..." Now that I had her on the phone, I didn't know what to say.

Missy seemed to pick up on my hesitancy and said, "Does this have anything to do with that person you like?"

She knew me too well. "Yeah," I said with resignation. "Of course."

"Okay, okay. Listen before you hit me with that, I think I've got an answer to that question you asked me a while ago."

"What's that?"

"The difference between seeing someone and going out."

"Oh, what's the difference?"

"Well, it's not exactly black and white."

What an interesting choice of words on Missy's part. "Kind of gray?" I suggested.

"Yeah, kind of gray. But I polled everybody in the dorm, and the consensus was that 'going out' with someone was a little more serious than 'seeing someone.' Seeing somebody isn't as intense; it's the beginning stages before formal dating."

"Okay, I get it."

"So," she singsonged, "is my baby sister *seeing* anyone?"

I took a deep breath. "Well, not really. I mean, we went out together with a bunch of friends, like you said, but we've never been, like, alone. And..."

"And you're still not sure if they like you. Is that it?"

"Yeah."

"Well, okay. You're in the same French class, right?"

"Yeah."

"Do you have anything else in common?"

"I don't know." I heard the uneasiness in my voice, and I'm sure Missy heard it, too.

"Okay, okay, squirt. What grade is sh—. What grade are they in?"

Oh, my God. Missy had almost said, "she." Oh, my God. Missy knows. Missy knows about me. I weighed my options for a split-second and figured since I was planning on telling her at some point, it may as well be now—on the phone—when I didn't have to see her reaction. I decided to go for it, and I said, "You know, don't you?"

"I wasn't sure."

"How long have you known?"

"Oh, I don't know. Maybe a year. I mean, c'mon, squirt, look at your side of the room. All your posters. And you never have any boys calling or coming over."

"Pretty obvious?"

"No, not really. I don't think Mom and Dad know."

"That's good."

"And I won't tell them."

I gasped. It felt like Missy had just punched me in the stomach. I hadn't once thought about Missy telling Mom and Dad about me. I couldn't even think about telling them right now. Someday, maybe, but not now.

"Thanks, Missy. I've got to figure all this out first before I tell them. You know?"

"Yeah, I understand. Look, I didn't even tell them when I first started going out with Kyle. Remember Kyle?"

"Yeah." I did remember him. Missy was in ninth grade. I was in fifth. Kyle was cute, but I didn't like him too much because he never wanted me along when they went to the movies or ice skating. I celebrated when she broke up with him over the summer. But I couldn't dwell on Missy's love life because I had to get to *my* problem before the sports banquet started.

"Missy, how do I know if...if she likes me?" Saying the words to Missy felt weird, but I guess my need for help with Rebecca was stronger than my fear of coming out to my sister. I should have been scared to death, but I wasn't for some reason.

"Well, first of all, if you don't mind telling me, who is this girl? Do I know her?"

"Kind of. Her name's Rebecca. She's a junior." I wasn't sure if I wanted to tell Missy who she was. I mean, I had just come out to my sister, and it felt like I was revealing my very soul.

"Rebecca...hmm. No, I don't think I know her. Wow. I'm glad you trust me with this. Okay, so do you and Rebecca have anything in common besides French?"

I thought about it for a second and realized that Rebecca and I did have something else in common. "Grandma," I said.

"Grandma?"

"Yeah, she..." I guess I had to tell Missy who she was, after all. "She's Mr. Washington's daughter."

"The funeral director?"

"Yeah."

"Oh, oh, oh! I know who you're talking about. She's gorgeous," she said as if she were impressed with me. "And her mom was gorgeous, too. Remember the Chinese bun she wore? You could wear your hair up like that, squirt. But, yeah, I remember Rebecca from the wake. Beautiful skin, amazing hair. So pretty. Way to go, squirt!"

I was blushing furiously. "Missy, cut it out."

"Sorry. But wow! Is she a lesbian, too?"

Lesbian. Missy had just called me and Rebecca lesbians. I wasn't sure I liked the label. I'd have to give that one a lot more thought. But not right now. I cleared my throat and said, "I don't know. I think, maybe. She seems to be pretty tight with this other girl, Jessie."

"Uh oh. Be careful. You like her, but it sounds like she's already in a relationship. Maybe you should walk away from this one for now."

"No!" I said way too loudly in the hotel lobby. A few girls looked in my direction, so I turned toward the wall and said low into the phone, "Missy, I can't. And they don't have a good relationship. Jessie's not good enough for her. She doesn't treat Rebecca right." I knew I was pleading, and it wasn't like Missy could make Jessie go away or anything.

"You're head over heels, aren't you, squirt? But Rebecca should be the one who decides who is and who isn't good enough for her. You know?"

"Yeah," I said with resignation. "I know, but..."

"But, hey. Nothing says you can't still hang out with her."

"Yeah."

"And get to know her better anyway, right?"

"Yeah." Now I knew why I had called my sister. She always said the right things.

"So, let's see. If Rebecca's family did Grandma's funeral, maybe you can ask her about that."

"Ask her what?"

"I don't know. It does seem kind of weird using Grandma this way."

I felt instant regret. "Yeah. Maybe we should find something else."

"No, no. I have an idea. You haven't been back to the cemetery, have you?"

"No."

"Does Rebecca drive?"

"I don't know. Jessie drives her around, so maybe not."

"Hmm, that could throw a monkey wrench into my idea."

I was getting impatient. "What idea?"

"With your learner's permit, you can't drive yourself, but maybe you can find out if she has her license. If she does, and this is the only way this is going to work, ask her if she'll take you there."

"To the cemetery?" It could work. Rebecca wouldn't invite Jessie along on something so obviously personal and private. I looked toward the front doors of the hotel and noticed that the steady stream of athletes had slowed way down. "Missy, I've got to go, but thanks for your help. And thanks for being cool about, you know, my news."

"Well, thanks for including me, dork, but now you have to give me regular updates."

"Like after tomorrow's field trip?" I knew Missy could hear my smile as I stood up and headed toward the ballroom.

"Oh, my God! You'll be with her all day?"

"Yeah. I know. I can't stand it, but I'll fill you in tomorrow." I said goodbye, took my smile, and headed to the girls' soccer table.

Chapter 8

The Field Trip

I never oversleep, but my alarm clock picked Tuesday of all days to screw up. It was the day of the St. Lawrence Seaway field trip. Breakfast would have to be the banana I grabbed off the counter as I ran by. I flung my backpack over both shoulders and ran the entire way to school. I know I must have looked pretty stupid running with my backpack bouncing around, but I couldn't miss the field trip. Rebecca would be there.

I almost leaped in ecstasy when I saw the two yellow school buses still parked in front of the school. Mme Depardieu was standing on the curb looking at her clipboard. I don't know how I did it, but I picked up speed and sprinted. She looked up and saw me. "Ah, Devon. Here you are. We were about to leave wizout you."

I blew out a breathless, "Sorry," and leaned over with my hands on my knees, trying to catch my breath.

She checked her clipboard and said, "Period eight is on bus two. Right here." She pointed to the second bus.

I stood up and took a deep breath. I didn't realize how out of shape I was. I vowed to run every single day from now on unless it was like ten below or blizzarding or something.

I stepped up into the bus and knew the chance of being able to sit with Rebecca was miniscule at that point. I just hoped I wouldn't have to sit in the front seat with Mme Depardieu. I reached the top step of the bus and said, "Sorry," to the bus driver. The older man reminded me of my grandfather with his snow-white hair and white mustache. He just nodded as if he couldn't care less and looked away. As I turned to survey the seating situation, somebody yelled, "Way to go, Devon." And then the entire busload of French language students started clapping. I shook my head and took an exaggerated bow. As I did so, I saw Rebecca wave at me. I couldn't believe my luck. The seat next to her was open.

I high-fived about ten kids on my fashionably late arrival as I made my way down the aisle. I whipped the hood of my sweat jacket off my head and threw my backpack on the floor. Just as I plopped down nonchalantly next to Rebecca, the bus started moving.

I smiled at her. "I can't believe I made it."

"Yeah, I was getting worried."

My heart warmed at the thought of Rebecca worrying about me. "My alarm clock didn't go off. I had to run all the way here."

"You ran?"

"Yeah."

"All the way?"

"And I discovered that I'm way out of shape."

"Not you," Rebecca said with a look of disbelief.

"I haven't been on a regular running schedule since..." I paused, not wanting to bring up the funeral again, but Rebecca finished my thought.

"Since your grandma?"

"Yeah."

"It takes time to get your normal routine back after something like that."

"Yeah." I drank in the softness in her eyes. "I'm finding that."

She smiled at me sympathetically.

I needed to change the subject fast before I got teary-eyed. "Did you save this seat for me?"

"Kind of. Well, I would have if anybody wanted to sit with me."

I couldn't fathom anyone *not* wanting to sit with Rebecca. God, she was so pretty. She even managed to make her bulky ski jacket look fashionable. Her fuzzy scarf looked so soft I wanted to reach out and touch it. How could the guys on this bus *not* have a crush on her like I did? "What do you mean?"

"No one ever wants to sit with me."

"What are you talking about? I want to sit with you." *Now and forever.*

Her eyes softened. "I know *you* do, but..."

"But what?" My stomach fluttered. She knew I wanted to sit with her.

"I don't know many of these kids." She looked away from me out the window at the passing cows.

I was confused, but at the same time, I was also pissed that my classmates had obviously hurt Rebecca's feelings somehow. I leaned in more closely and asked softly, "Why do you think no one wants to sit with you?"

"You don't know?"

I furiously scanned my brain but came up empty. "No."

"Devon, look around this bus."

I stretched in my seat and looked around at my classmates. They were the same kids I'd been going to school with since forever. A lot of them since kindergarten, but practically all of them since middle school.

"I don't—"

"You're looking, but you're not seeing." She looked at me with such a serious expression that I felt really stupid for missing something that was apparently uber obvious. She pulled up the sleeve of her ski jacket and revealed her forearm. She gestured for me to do the same. She placed her deep velvet skin next to my winter pale skin. She touched her forearm and then touched mine. My heart almost stopped when she touched me, but I tried to ignore it as meaning flooded my brain cells. Her skin was darker than everybody else's, including mine. She was the only Black kid on the bus.

I looked into her eyes and saw such a deep sadness in them that I felt guilty. Guilty that I was white and that once upon a time, I probably ignored her just like my classmates had done that morning. I reached over, grabbed her bare forearm, and gave it a reassuring squeeze. I hoped she understood my gesture to mean that I didn't condone my classmates' actions and that I was in her corner.

She pulled her sleeve back down, and I did the same. I had no idea what to say, so we both looked out her window as we paralleled the Grasse River on its path toward Massena. The once-green corn fields across the river were already tucked away for winter. I had told Missy there were two main obstacles in reaching Rebecca. One—I didn't know if Rebecca was into girls, and two--I didn't know if she was with Jessie. But maybe I had a third obstacle. Maybe Rebecca thought I would be prejudiced against her or something just because I was white like the rest of the kids on the bus.

As the bus passed the entrance to the Eisenhower Lock and headed into the short tunnel toward the power dam, I decided to ignore all my worries and focus on spending a nice day with Rebecca.

Once through the tunnel, the bus made a right turn onto a narrow two-lane road toward the power dam. Without looking at me, Rebecca tapped me on the arm. "Look! Look! See the bird?" She pointed to a bright red woodpecker on an old dead tree.

"That's cool." I smiled at her and was happy she wanted to share the woodpecker with me. I didn't tell her that the bird was a pileated woodpecker because I didn't want to seem like some kind of birdbrain nerd. Maybe sometime I'd talk to her about birds and other nature stuff—like my ideas about the environment. That's why I was kind of psyched about going to the dam. Maybe we could talk about hydroelectric power and other ways to be green, but I didn't care what we talked about, actually, because I was just happy to spend the day with her and two busloads of our classmates.

When the bus pulled to a stop in front of the Robert Moses-Robert H. Saunders Dam, I stood up first but let Rebecca walk in front of me. My pulse soared when she looked back at me with a grateful expression on her face. Oh, yeah, I had just scored another point. Go me.

The two busloads of students filled the lobby of the visitors' center. My stomach growled as soon as I walked in because the smell of popcorn was overwhelming. The guides introduced themselves and divided our mass into four groups. I made sure Rebecca and I were in the same group but was bummed because our group got assigned to the far end of the hands-on exhibit room. I was bummed because you could only eat the popcorn in the lobby, and my stomach protested this little rule quite loudly.

We gathered around the picture window overlooking the dam, and Rebecca stayed glued to my side. Or maybe it was I who remained glued to hers. Either way, I kind of felt like her protector, but I stopped short of puffing out my chest and strutting like a rooster. I was proud to have Rebecca as my friend, and I was sorry that it took the death of my grandmother for me to realize what a great person she was.

Our guide introduced himself as John. He looked like a college guy, probably about Missy's age. I felt bad for him. I bet he hated giving tours to high school kids.

John pointed toward the St. Lawrence River just outside the window. "This, as you know, is the St. Lawrence. To get to the visitors' center today, you went through the tunnel under the Eisenhower Lock. The reason the ships go through the lock is because the power dam blocks off the only other potential route in this area."

I remembered the few times I'd seen the humongous ships go through the locks. They needed the locks to help them navigate the changing water heights of the St. Lawrence River on their way west toward the Great Lakes or east toward Québec and the Atlantic Ocean.

Rebecca and I moved closer to the window, and I said low enough for only Rebecca to hear, "Dam," as if I was impressed with the power dam outside the window. She giggled at my joke but covered her mouth with a hand so no one would hear. I heard, of course, and my perma-grin emerged instantly.

Actually, the power dam was impressive. I knew from other field trips that it connected the U.S. with Canada and was a joint project between both countries. If more countries cooperated like that, some of the world's problems might just get solved. I laughed at myself because I didn't remember doing this kind of deep thinking the last time I was here back in fourth grade.

John leaned against the wall near the windows and said, "Now, before we move on to the exhibits behind you, I want to give you a quick history of the river. Jacques Cartier was a French navigator who had been searching for a western route from Europe to Asia—the elusive northwest passage—and in 1535, he found this river that led into the heart of the North American continent. When he first discovered the Gulf of the St. Lawrence, he named the northern shore *Canada*, so Cartier is thought to have discovered Canada."

I whispered to Rebecca, "Yeah, he *discovered* Canada just like Columbus *discovered* America."

She suppressed another giggle and nudged me in the arm with her elbow.

"Ack," I said way too loudly. A couple of the kids right in front of us turned around, and that made us laugh even more. I had to look away from her so I wouldn't crack up completely.

John continued. "The name Canada, or Kanata—spelled K-A-N-A-T-A— is actually a Huron-Iroquois word meaning village. And, of course, the native peoples, the Iroquois in particular, were quite surprised to find the big ships as far inland as Québec."

Rebecca nudged me again, and I shrugged as if to say, "Okay, okay, so he knew about the native Americans." Or should they be called native Canadians? John called them the native people. I decided not to embarrass myself by asking.

"Ah, Québec," Mme Depardieu said brightly. *"C'est là où se trouve le pont de Jacques Cartier, n'est-ce pas?"*

When John looked at her with a confused expression, she laughed and said, *"Pardon.* Québec is zeh home of zee Jacques Cartier Bridge, *oui?"*

"Oh," he said with such obvious relief that his reaction made us laugh. "Yes, the Jacques Cartier Bridge crosses right over the St. Lawrence River in Montréal, but Canada doesn't have the only claim on Cartier. The Cartier State Park, right here in the U.S., borders the St. Lawrence in Morrisville, just west of Ogdensburg."

Mme Depardieu had the biggest smile on her face that I'd ever seen. John seemed to pick up on the fact that she was a Jacques Cartier fan and asked, "Is this the French class field trip?" He looked all of us over.

"Oui, of course. We're from Grasse River High School." Mme Depardieu beamed again, but this time, her look included all of us. I took satisfaction in her smile because she was obviously proud of us. I definitely felt a lot different on this field trip than in fourth grade.

"Oh, Grasse River. Here's an interesting fact for you," John continued. "The Eisenhower Lock used to be referred to as the Grasse River Lock."

That was kind of cool. Our little river was famous. I decided to put my reporter hat on. Maybe I'd propose an article for the Gazette about Mme Depardieu's annual mecca to the land of Jacques Cartier. I raised my hand high in the air and hoped I didn't sound like a jerk asking my simple question.

"Yes?" Ranger John pointed at me. "In the back?"

"Do you know when the lock was built?" I knew we were at the power dam and *not* at the lock, but John seemed interested, so what could it hurt to ask?

"Good question. I'll go ahead and detour on that topic for a second, but then I must get us back to the power dam stuff, or they won't let me have popcorn."

A couple of the girls in the front giggled.

"Well," he continued, "the lock officially opened in 1959. You all remember 1959, don't you?" The girls giggled again when he looked at them. "No? Okay, well, President Dwight Eisenhower and Queen Elizabeth were both on the first ceremonial ship through the lock, but it was New York Governor Roosevelt—Franklin Delano Roosevelt, that is—that was the first one to push for the lock."

I knew that Roosevelt had been governor of New York State, but I had no idea that FDR, as my Grandma called him, had even cared about the North Country.

John continued, "Roosevelt wanted the locks for defense purposes so we could protect our military ships in the Seaway in the event of war. The cost was enormous, and most people didn't see the need for the locks or a seaway from the Atlantic to the Great Lakes. Roosevelt persevered, though, even from the White House. He died in 1945. President Eisenhower gave the lock the final push, and it was finished in 1959. The lock was named for him."

I felt kind of bad for President Roosevelt at that moment, but at least he'd had the power project named after him.

John smiled at me and said, "Okay, the history part is finished and now your tour turns into science."

He asked us to stay on one side of the exhibit hall and briefly explained some of the exhibits we'd see along the way. Most of the exhibits were hands-on, and he encouraged us to read the signs and try everything out.

"Try to understand the underlying physics behind each exhibit," he told us as he set us free. "Fourth graders just turn the knobs and press the buttons without understanding. This is your chance to get it this time. You have about twenty minutes on this side, and then once Marcy's group is out of the way, we'll continue up the other side."

Rebecca and I turned toward the exhibits.

"I wish we could have gone to the lock today, too," I said, "It's kind of cool."

"Yeah, it is," Rebecca agreed and smiled at me in a way that made my knees wobble. "It's too cold today, but maybe we can go there next summer.

We can watch some ships go through. Jessie hates stuff like that."

Another point for me. Take that, Jessie. Of course, I didn't say any of this out loud. I just smiled and said, "That'd be fun. And then we'll go fishing, right?"

"Absolutely." She nudged me lightly with her elbow again. "Are you still coming to my dance concert?"

"Yeah, of course. Three weeks from this Friday." I knew the date of her dance concert by heart.

"Yeah, right before Christmas. Ooh, Devon, I'm sorry."

I had no idea what she was sorry about. We were looking at an exhibit about transformers, but I couldn't see why transformers would make her apologize. "Sorry about what?"

"I brought up Christmas."

"Oh." A quick wave of sadness overtook me, but I fought hard to let it go. "That's okay." I took a deep breath and exhaled slowly. "Tomorrow, it'll be one month."

"Already?"

"Yeah, and on Christmas day—two months."

"On Christmas Day. Oh, that sucks." She put a hand on the sleeve of my jean jacket in sympathy. "That's going to be a hard day for you."

I saw my opening and silently thanked Missy for the idea. "Yeah, and I haven't been back to visit her yet." I looked down but watched her out of the corner of my eye.

"Oh, you haven't?"

I almost got lost in her soft, brown, sympathetic eyes, but I gathered up my courage and threw out the bait. "No, I only have my permit. And I don't have a car anyway." I held my breath and hoped she would go for it.

"Oh, Devon. You should have asked me. I can drive you. I got my license in September. And if the cemetery's locked, I can get the key."

"You can?" I remembered to breathe again and wished I could hug her.

"Of course I can. Now, this week—Thanksgiving—is a little busy. My Aunt Lucinda, my mom's sister, is coming up from Plymouth and spending the whole four-day weekend with us. I'll be lucky if I can sneak away for the basketball games on Friday and Saturday."

"I hope you can," I said way too quickly.

"I think so. My mom knows that Jessie's my best friend."

Best friend. Is that all, Rebecca, or is it more than that?

"But," she continued, "maybe we can go visit your Grandma sometime next week after school. Okay?"

"Okay. Thank you." I wanted to say more, like how kind it was of her, but it sounded too cheesy. My brain moved on to other things, anyway, like Jessie. Somehow, I doubted Jessie was just a friend, but I didn't know how to get Rebecca to tell me. Rebecca had to know that I liked her. How could she not? How could anybody who saw the way I looked at her *not* know I was falling in love with her? Well, maybe it wasn't love because I didn't really know what love was, but it was definitely stronger than anything I felt for Marcy Berger and all those other crushes I'd had along the way.

We walked on silently, and I pretended to be fascinated by the old photographs of all the dams on the St. Lawrence River. I let Rebecca lead the way through the exhibit hall, and I almost laughed out loud because on the night Jessie stranded me at Bruster, I had decided that I would follow Rebecca wherever she led, and here I was, following her around on our field trip.

She stopped in front of a photograph of President Nixon and Queen Elizabeth. "What's so funny?" she asked.

"Nothing." I looked down at my feet.

"No, c'mon. I saw you smile."

What was I supposed to say, that I wanted to follow her everywhere? I made up something quick. "I was thinking how Mme Depardieu drags us out here in November because she just loves Jacques Cartier. And he had nothing to do with the Seaway. I mean, not really."

"She's funny about things like that, isn't she?" She flashed me a mischievous smile, and the mirth in her eyes made me smile even more.

"Yeah." Oh, what a conversationalist I was. My brain was mush. Couldn't I think of anything more clever to say than *yeah*?

"Hey, Devon?"

"Yeah?"

"Are you sure you're okay hanging out with me today?"

I couldn't believe she was asking me that question. "Yeah. Why?"

82

"Oh, well. I just…you know." She pulled up her sleeve again and showed me her forearm.

Of course, it didn't matter to me that her skin color was darker than mine. But no. The thought didn't sit right with me. Her skin color did matter. She obviously felt alienated from our classmates because of it. Her skin color and heritage were part of what made her the person she was. Even though we lived in the same town, her life and experiences seem to have been vastly different than mine. I wanted to ask her about that. The only thing I could think to say was, "I'm sorry people haven't been kind to you. Maybe we can talk about that sometime?"

She didn't respond right away. She studied my face as if looking for something—my sincerity, maybe? After a moment, she sighed and said, "Well, I just don't want you getting any grief from—" She twirled her hand around, indicating the other students in the exhibit hall.

"Them? Pfft. Don't worry about them. Who cares what they think?"

"Well, it's kind of hard being different."

Was she trying to feel me out on the race issue? I wasn't sure, but I tried to make her feel better by saying, "Well, I kind of know what it's like to be different." Not that anybody knew I was different since I wasn't out of the closet yet, but still.

"No, I don't think you do, Devon."

"Yeah, actually, I do. Your difference is just a little more, uh, obvious."

She was about to say something, but then a bunch of our classmates came by, so we had to drop the subject. And even though I had just kind of come out to her, we managed to walk on for a while in what I would call a comfortable silence.

John directed our group to the other side of the exhibits and then later to the movie in the big theater. I could hardly concentrate on the movie with Rebecca sitting so close to me in the semi-darkness. Of course, I finally got to have popcorn while watching the short videos. After I wolfed my bag of popcorn down, Rebecca did the most amazing thing and held her bag out toward me. I whispered a thank you and took a dainty amount. Rebecca simply nodded and turned her attention back to the video. Something, I don't know what it was, flushed over my entire body. I silently wished my classmates to disappear but was completely unsuccessful. I was also unsuccessful getting the heat to leave my face. I know I was blushing furiously when the lights came back on. Had Rebecca seen? I had no clue what she must have been thinking.

We walked back out to the lobby, and I couldn't believe it when Monsieur LaFrett, the other French teacher, announced that we had to get back on the busses to return to school. It felt like we had just gotten there.

Rebecca and I walked together to the bus, and I stepped aside to let her get on first. She seemed surprised by my chivalry, and I couldn't help but think that Jessie would have bounded on the bus, leaving Rebecca trailing behind. I heard the scoreboard tick over again. Another point for me.

She headed toward the same seat we had shared earlier and slid all the way to the window. I sat next to her, but sitting this close made my palms sweat and my stomach go flippy. I tried to act normal, but that was nearly impossible. I felt better once the bus started moving back toward the tunnel to Massena.

Rebecca turned to me and asked, "Did you bring lunch?"

I smiled at her, kept eye contact, and reached down for my backpack. I unzipped the front pouch and smiled as I pulled out the banana that was supposed to have been my breakfast. I held it up in all its glory for her to see.

"That's it? A banana?" She looked at me incredulously.

"Faulty alarm clock, remember?"

"Oh, you didn't have time." Her eyes were an odd mixture of sympathy and laughter.

"I'm lucky I got this baby." I wiggled the banana and then zipped it back into my backpack.

"I'll share if you want. I've got plenty. My mom made my lunch, and she packed me a huge turkey sandwich on seven-grain bread with…" She opened her lunch bag and rooted around. "Oh, a granola bar and some carrots. I could split them. Sound okay to you?"

I got all jiggly inside thinking that Rebecca wanted to share her lunch with me. I had planned to snag half of Gail's sandwich, but maybe Rebecca wanted me to eat lunch with her at the same table and everything. "Thanks. Looks like your mom knew I'd be in a pickle today."

Rebecca made a show of looking in her lunch bag again. "Nope, no pickles." She chuckled at her own joke. Laughing with her felt amazing.

84

"Well, that's okay," I said. "I'm not a pickle fan anyway."

"Me neither. I'll take the original cucumber instead."

"Oh, I know. Me, too." We settled into a conversation about the foods we liked, and it turned out that we both liked to eat fairly healthily, but she admitted a weakness for hot fudge brownie sundaes. For me, it was black raspberry ice cream with chocolate sprinkles. We decided that we would pig out at Scoopalicous once they reopened in the spring.

We were almost through the tunnel when the bus swerved wildly. I flew into Rebecca, and we both put our hands down on the seat between us to brace ourselves. Our hands touched. She didn't move hers. I didn't move mine. I didn't look at her as I reached over and linked my pinky with hers.

Chapter 9

A Sucky Day

Thanksgiving without Grandma was kind of sucky. Uncle Joe sat in Grandma's usual spot next to Dad, and I couldn't help but think that Uncle Joe had just moved up in the family pecking order. Families change, I realized. Families shift. Grandmas die. I squeezed my eyes shut at the dinner table so I wouldn't cry in front of everybody. I made myself think about Rebecca and holding her pinky on the bus. That helped me keep it together a little.

My cousin Jarrod pretty much ignored everybody, and after dinner, he sat in the living room with his headphones blasting some kind of heavy metal music. He was in tenth grade at Grasse River, but even though he and I were related, I never hung out with him. We were from two different worlds. Everybody was always amazed when they found out we were cousins. Mom used to make me hang out with him, but since he was so antisocial, she gave me permission to retreat to my room after I had cleared the table.

I went up to my room and tried not to notice Grandma's open bedroom door. I left the lights off and flung myself on the bed. I hugged Grizzly as hard as I could and cried as I remembered Dad's grace before the meal. He'd started by saying, "Thanksgiving is a time to give thanks, and I would like to thank the Lord for the wonderful life He gave my mother—" He glanced at Uncle Joe and modified his toast. "—*our* mother a good life. We were lucky to be able to call her Mom or Grandma." When he said "Grandma," I started crying for real. I think Missy did, too, because she wiped her eyes a couple of times. I bowed my head even more and hoped I wouldn't embarrass myself by having to leave the table or something. I saw my mom rest her hand on Dad's wrist while he spoke. I thought that was sweet and was glad that we had such a boring, normal family that could comfort each other, but I was incredibly glad when we got to say, "Amen."

We tried to make Thanksgiving seem like every other, but I, for one, had a hard time pulling it off. I kept thinking little things about Grandma, like how she hated green bean casserole. She always said the mushroom soup ruined perfectly good green beans. I wondered if my mom or dad would ever have to live with me or with Missy when they got older, like Grandma had lived with us. Would I say grace someday and thank the Lord for the life of my mom or my dad?

I lay on my bed in the dark and tried to convince myself that Grandma was the major reason I wanted to go to the cemetery with Rebecca next week. I tried but failed and felt like the biggest jerk. Being with Rebecca was the major reason. Maybe we could hold pinky fingers again. Or, hey, maybe we could even go all the way and hold hands. I scoffed out loud but suppressed my smile because I needed to make visiting Grandma my priority. I think I was kind of scared going to the cemetery, though. I wasn't sure how emotional I would get, and I didn't want to embarrass myself in front of Rebecca again.

On the bus, I had just taken advantage of a good thing—thanks to my grandfather-look-alike bus driver swerving to avoid a workman changing light bulbs in the tunnel. Grabbing her pinky was my way of giving her a sign. She was probably thinking, "Finally!" Well, either that or "Ewww!"

And it might just be the second thing because she still hadn't called or texted me since the field trip. Did I text or call her? No, I was too scared. After the field trip, she handed me half her lunch and then hurried into the school building, leaving me behind. By the time I got to the cafeteria, she was already sitting with Jessie and her regular group of friends. I tried hard not to be disappointed as I made my way toward Gail and Joey.

Even though Rebecca ditched me after the field trip, she asked me during French class later that day if I was going to the basketball game on Friday.

"You bet," I'd said and cringed at how dorky it sounded.

I couldn't read her intentions for asking me if I was going. Was that her way of telling me that she had kind of been okay with our pinky fingers touching? Had she been holding my pinky right back? It felt like it. But maybe she asked if I was going so she could steer clear of me. Realization dawned on me as I sank into my bed. Maybe she wasn't going to go to the game because I was going. Either way, I'd find out in less than twenty-four hours. If she didn't show or if she was cold to me, then I'd take the hint and back off. I'd pretend I didn't have a major crush on her. I'd pretend she didn't make me lose my breath whenever I saw her. I'd pretend just like I'd been pretending ever since my crush on Marcy Berger began.

I wished she would just lose Jessie once and for all and be with me. Don't people lose their kids at the mall all the time? Jessie liked to go to the mall. Why couldn't Rebecca just take her there, drop her off, and lose her?

I rolled my eyes and hugged Grizzly. I looked at Missy's bed. She came home Wednesday night. She told me that she would move back into her old room when she came home for Christmas. Between now and then, she and Mom had to figure out what to do with all of Grandma's stuff. I was one thousand percent relieved that I wasn't asked to be part of the decision-making. Mom would probably donate her clothes to some kind of non-profit thrift store or something. I don't know what they were going to do with her other things. Grandma had a lot of knick-knacks. I hoped Mom would let me keep the New York City snow globe, but then again, Missy would probably want that back. I'd have to ask Missy before she went back to school on Sunday.

I heard my aunt and uncle and my anti-social cousin Jarrod leaving. When the front door closed and their car engine started up, I jumped into my PJs, even though it was only eight o'clock. Friday would come more quickly this way.

~~~

The Grasse River girls' basketball team had an early five-point lead over Jefferson High School. The scoreboard clock showed 1:52 left to play in the first quarter. When I got to the gym, just before game time, I looked for Rebecca in the bleachers. She was there, all right, sitting with a lot of the same kids she sat with at lunch. I didn't know her friends' names, which made me feel kind of stupid because our school wasn't that big. Not really. We only had about three hundred and fifty students in each class. I tried to make eye contact with her, but I got the distinct feeling she was deliberately ignoring me. Her indifference hurt my heart. I guess I'd gotten my answer. I took the hint and made my way toward the middle of the bleachers, smack in between the Jefferson and the Grasse River fans. I had my reporter's notebook out and jotted down notes now and then. I was not sports-minded, so my notes were just words the fans, players, and coaches shouted. Nothing about this game made sense, just like Rebecca. Nothing about her made sense, either. Obviously, she hadn't been counting down every minute until she could see me again, like the way I had.

Every now and then, I'd sneak a peek her way, but she seemed totally riveted by the game. And riveted by all the guys surrounding her, too. I knew there had to be somebody at this school who liked her as much as I did. The guys, all of them, were Black. In fact, everybody sitting around Rebecca was Black. Maybe I should have just walked up the bleacher steps and sat down next to her. But then again, maybe she wasn't like me. Maybe I needed to shut up and try to make sense of this basketball game.

I tried to take more notes on the game, but I wasn't very successful. To distract myself, I opened the tournament program. It listed the rosters for each team, and I saw that Jessie was one of two seniors. Belinda Carmichael was the other. I'd interview Belinda after the game, and even though I should interview Jessie, too, it'd be a warm day in a North Country winter before that happened.

The game was pretty fast-paced, and it was obvious that Jessie liked to run. I hated to admit it, but she was good. Natalie played pretty well, too, but Jessie was undeniably the best player on the Grasse River team. I watched as the Jefferson team missed a shot, and Natalie jumped up and grabbed the ball after it careened off the backboard.

"Nice rebound." I heard someone say. *Oh, so that's a rebound.* I'd heard the word before, but I couldn't quite remember what it was.

Natalie then threw the ball to Jessie, who had taken off running toward the Grasse River basket. Jessie caught the ball on the run, dribbled a couple of times, and bounced it gently off the backboard. The ball went through the net, and I heard someone say, "Sweet lay-up." When we were at the mall, Jessie had mentioned something about making a lay-up as soft as a baby's butt or something, and I guess that's what she'd just done.

When the buzzer finally sounded for halftime, the Grasse River team was ahead by a score of 32-24. I kind of wanted to leave, but Mom and Missy were going to start on Grandma's room tonight while I was at the game. Missy kind of hinted that they knew it would be upsetting for me to witness it, so I simply stayed rooted to my spot on the hard bleachers as the other fans stood up and milled about. I eavesdropped on conversations around me trying to drink in anything and everything basketball. I learned that rebounds, steals, and something called assists were important statistics. I guess I should have learned those terms in P.E., but since it wasn't that important to me then, I didn't remember anything. And turnovers, I learned, were not a good thing. Someone in the stands thought that Jessie had more turnovers than usual. Somehow, I'd have to find out what exactly that was. I shook my head at my ignorance. How could Mrs. Gibson think I could be a sports editor? Sure, I knew how to put words together, but it was becoming obvious that I knew next to nothing about sports.

I stood up and stretched, and while doing so, I tried to find Rebecca with my peripheral vision. God, she was pretty. No, she was beautiful. She had her hair pulled back into a ponytail, which lay softly against her green turtleneck sweater. Her long skirt made her look elegant—even sitting in the bleachers at a basketball game. Her long gold earrings dangled deliciously near her neck, and I had to look away. God, she made my insides gooey. I looked away for another reason, though. One of the guys sitting near her caught me staring. I was wrong about her, wasn't I? Maybe what I thought were signs weren't. Maybe Rebecca was as straight as they came and had only been nice to me because of Grandma.

I sighed and opened my reporter's notebook. I wrote Rebecca's name in big block letters and then, with a frown, put a line through it. I was barking up the wrong tree, I guess. I closed my notebook and settled back to watch the little kids shooting baskets on the court. I had to close my eyes, though. A deluge of feelings about Rebecca flooded my brain and body. I had to find a way to get her out of my head.

I couldn't believe how many things I'd done today that were motivated by Rebecca. Since I had gone to bed so early on Thanksgiving night, I woke up at five in the morning. I tried to go back to sleep, but after rolling around for half an hour, I just got up. Luckily, my sweatshirt and running shoes were still on the floor by my bed, so I managed to get dressed without waking up Missy. I snuck out the front door and went for a run in the dark. My mom would have killed me if she'd known, but I had vowed to run every day. As I ran, I realized that Rebecca was my main motivation. I wanted to look good for her. When I got home, I turned on the kitchen light and poured myself some of my mom's healthy cereal—some kind of bran flakes or something. I wanted to eat better today, too, because I had kind of pigged out on Thanksgiving.

After my shower, I ironed my shirt, and then I ironed my jeans, even though Missy teased me about it. I put my hair up and then put on my hoop earrings. I was ready to go to the game by eleven that morning, even though it didn't even start until seven in the evening. Oh, I wanted to text Rebecca so bad, but I restrained myself and channeled my energy into doing homework. That lasted all of five minutes, though, so I switched on my computer. I googled Rebecca's name, but the only thing I found was a newspaper article about the dance troupe's concert from last spring. Her name was listed as one of the dancers, but that was the only mention of her. Missy walked into our room when I was doing that, and she demanded her update. I told her about the pinky thing on the bus, and she told me that I had a set of brass ones.

Sitting alone on the hard bleachers at the basketball game, I realized that maybe I scared Rebecca away. We had so much fun hanging out during the field trip, but at the basketball game, she seemed completely uninterested and cold. Talk about mixed messages.

When the teams came back on the court for the third quarter from wherever they had disappeared, I was relieved because I could focus on something other than Rebecca. I don't know what the Jefferson team did to get motivated during halftime, but they scored six points in a row while Grasse River scored nothing. I learned that the correct way to phrase this was, "Six unanswered points." I jotted that down in my notebook, along with a thousand other basketball phrases.

When I looked back up toward the game, Rebecca was making her way up the bleachers toward me. Like an idiot, I forgot to breathe. I only noticed it because my lungs demanded air. And then I felt like a bigger idiot for inhaling so loudly. I slid over on the wooden bleacher so she could sit down.

"Hey, at least we're still winning, right?" I gestured toward the game.

She sat down without touching me. "Yeah, but Jessie had better start playing some defense, or we're gonna get creamed."

"I have to be honest. I don't know what I'm looking at." I gestured toward the court. "I mean, I should know as the sports editor, but, well…" I shrugged.

Rebecca laughed, that cool laugh that made my insides smile. "Well, what I usually do is find a player to watch for a while."

And that would be Jessie, I thought sarcastically.

She continued. "Like Belinda. She's boxing out better than usual and getting more rebounds. And she's even got more points than Jessie, I think."

"Okay, you lost me at boxing out."

She laughed again and said, "Okay. Let's watch Belinda. No, don't watch the ball, just watch Belinda."

Our team was on defense, and Belinda stuck like glue to the tall Jefferson player she defended. Another Jefferson player took a shot, and Belinda spun around and stuck her butt in the other girl's stomach. I raised my eyebrows and almost laughed, but then she jumped with perfect timing to grab the ball as it bounced off the rim.

"That," Rebecca said, smiling at me, "is boxing out."

"Wow." I was impressed.

"Yeah, Belinda's good. But after I follow a player around for a while, I look at the other team and try to figure out what defense they're using. Like, look," she pointed down the court where Jessie dribbled the ball, "See how each Jefferson player kind of defends a certain area on the court? Watch Natalie cut through the key. See how no one stayed with her all the way? That's a zone defense."

"Did you play basketball?" I opened my notebook, making sure I didn't open to the page where I had crossed out her name and jotted down "zone defense." I also wrote the word "key." I learned more vocabulary in an hour of watching basketball than I had all year in Mme Depardieu's French class.

"Well, yeah, I played basketball in middle school, but then the dance thing took over full-time."

"You know a lot."

She laughed. "I know so much because I've watched Jessie play since, oh, I don't know, forever."

Since forever? I swallowed hard and said, "I've just been watching the ball go up and down the court."

She looked at me with her soft eyes and said, "Yeah, well, when you go to as many games as I do, you have to find some way to keep it interesting."

Before I could stop myself, I asked, "Do you watch Jessie?"

She snorted and rolled her eyes. "I used to."

I stayed quiet, hoping she'd elaborate, but she didn't. My reporter tricks didn't work on her, I guess. I wished she'd say something about the school bus and holding pinkies. But she didn't, and neither did I.

We watched the game in silence for a few moments, and then she stood up abruptly, announcing that she had to get back.

"You do?" Even I heard the disappointment in my voice.

"Yeah, my friends are probably wondering where I've gone." She gestured to the group of Black kids, most of whom were watching the game, but then I noticed a couple of them look in our direction.

"Okay." I didn't know how to make her stay. She started down the steps when I surprised myself by blurting, "Rebecca."

She turned around. "Yeah?"

"Can we go see my grandma? Next week?"

"Oh, yeah. I didn't forget. I'll figure something out. See you later." She turned away from me and made her way back to her friends. I felt like I had just been dismissed.

If she had asked me to sit with her and her friends, I would have moved in an instant. It wasn't like I owned this minuscule patch of bleacher or anything. I think she just didn't want her friends to meet me. Or she didn't want me to meet her friends. Either way, I was confused.

As miserable as I was, I decided to make it worse by watching Jessie play. She dribbled the ball up the court and passed it to Natalie. Jessie ran through the key past Belinda and popped out on the other side. Natalie leaped up and whizzed the ball all the way over to Jessie, who caught it and then took a jump shot. "Jump shot" was one of the new phrases I learned that night. The ball bounced off the backboard so hard that even a few of the Grasse River fans laughed. I felt kind of bad for her, but at the same time, I had a ha-ha feeling about it.

I continued to watch Jessie play as the Jefferson team dribbled the ball back up toward its own basket. Jessie followed Jefferson player #12 around the floor, and when another Jefferson player took a shot, Jessie turned to do one of those box-out moves. She spun around and made contact with #12 just like Belinda had done earlier, but then she jammed her elbow into the girl's side. I don't know a lot about the game, but I was pretty sure that was illegal. A foul or something. It had to be, but the referees didn't blow the whistle, so maybe jamming someone with your elbow was okay.

Things continued to go bad for Jessie as the game went on. She only scored four points during the entire second half, but luckily for us, Belinda played well, and we won. I don't think I ever would have noticed what a dirty player Jessie was if Rebecca hadn't shown me how to watch a basketball game. I wonder if Rebecca taught me that trick, knowing I would watch Jessie and see how mean she was. But, believe me, I already knew how mean she was.

As I walked out of the gym, Missy was waiting in her car to pick me up. I didn't know what kind of update I was going to give her because Rebecca was incredibly confusing. This had been another sucky day.

Chapter 10

Brown and Beige

The Kinney drugstore wasn't crowded on Sunday, which was good because I wasn't in the mood for people, anyway. My mom was at the pharmacy getting some kind of prescription filled while I wandered around the store. Missy had already gone back to Plattsburgh, and I needed a distraction from my life, so I jumped at the chance when Mom asked me to go to Kinney's with her.

I planted myself in front of the magazines and looked at all the covers. No Jessica Alba today. Maybe she'd make another movie, and I could get a new magazine. I sighed. No Rebecca, either. She had been so weird at the basketball game on Friday night that I wasn't surprised when she treated me like a chore at the tournament finals on Saturday. She did come over and say hello, though, but she acted as if it was her duty or something. I think she didn't want to be seen with me because she kept sneaking peeks at Jessie and then at her group of friends as if anxious to get away from me.

I wandered over to the perfume section at Kinney's and looked for anything with a rose scent. That was Rebecca's fragrance. I picked up a pump spray bottle named "Rose Petals." I squirted a little on my wrist and then rubbed both wrists together. The scent was a little strong at first, but as I waved my wrists around, the scent of roses took me to the middle of a garden teaming with plush red roses in full bloom. Rebecca, of course, walked with me in the garden, and we stopped now and then to take in the intoxicating fragrance.

I exhaled and decided that I didn't care if my mom made fun of me, but I was going to make her buy me the body spray. I never bought perfumes or body sprays, and she'd probably wonder what was wrong with me, but I really didn't care if she thought I was losing my mind because maybe I was a little.

95

I practically floated away from the perfume section and found myself in the toy aisle. Missy and I used to play board games. And cards. We used to play Go *Fish* all the time, then *War,* and I think the last game we were hooked on was *Gin Rummy.* Even Mom played with us sometimes. Maybe I'd challenge Mom to a gin rummy game when we got home. I smiled at myself because I knew I was just looking for comfort. I'd make a great psychologist someday. Too bad I was going to be an environmental journalist.

As I rounded the corner to check out the toys on the back wall, I noticed a bin filled with tiny stuffed animals. They were cute the way real puppies were cute. All fuzzy and innocent. Maybe I should get one so Grizzly wouldn't be lonely. Ah, but then again, Grizzly might get jealous. Best not to hurt my teddy bear's feelings. I picked up a panda bear with the cutest furry face from the bin. She was so cute that I gave her a quick hug. I hoped nobody was watching because here I was, a sixteen-year-old girl, a junior in high school, hugging a stuffed toy in the drugstore. I was about to put the cutie pie back in the overcrowded bin when something made me pull her back out again. Her colors were black and white like Rebecca and me. Well, I wasn't exactly white—more like beige or something. And Rebecca wasn't exactly black in color, either. She was more like brown. So, we weren't actually black and white at all, were we? We were brown and beige.

I started to walk away from the toys, but then I had my nine-thousandth epiphany since meeting Rebecca. Maybe Jessie told her she shouldn't hang out with me, the "white girl." Maybe Jessie got mad if Rebecca didn't hang out with their crowd—the Black kids. The *brown* kids, I thought with a grin. Or maybe it was her friends who gave her grief for hanging out with me. Either way, it sucked. But I was sure Rebecca didn't have a problem with me as a beige-American. Of course, maybe I wore rose-colored glasses, but then everyone would be rose in color. Aha, everyone should wear rose-colored glasses, and then we'd all be the same color.

I decided to somehow have this exact conversation with Rebecca. I'd give her the panda bear to show her that black and white could coexist in harmony or something just as corny, but then maybe I'd launch into my rose-colored glasses theory. Maybe. If I ever had the chance to really talk to her again, which I kind of doubted.

~~~

On Monday afternoon, I sat in my usual seat in French class, and Rebecca sat next to me in what had become her usual seat, but we barely spoke to each other. I wasn't sure what had happened between us because we had laughed so much on the field trip. I guess the pinky incident, the pinky debacle, the pinky scandal had freaked her out. But she didn't seem to mind on the bus. She would have pulled away if she was freaked out, wouldn't she? I decided firmly that Rebecca was very confusing.

I had the black and white panda bear in my backpack, and I desperately wanted to give it to her, but she wasn't exactly sending me friendly vibes. How could I go into my new theories if she wasn't speaking to me? I felt like we were in the middle of a fight or something, but I had no clue what we were fighting about.

Mme Depardieu finished the lesson for the day and, after thanking us for our "wonderful behavior" on the St. Lawrence field trip, asked us to start our sentence translation homework, but I decided that I needed to talk to Rebecca instead. My French homework could wait until after the rifle match at the shooting gallery later that afternoon.

I listened to the sound of Rebecca's pen as she did her assignment. I hated to interrupt her, but I had to. I needed some kind of contact.

"Hey, Rebecca?" I whispered.

She looked up from her work. "Yeah?"

"That was a good game against Unionville Saturday, wasn't it?"

"Oh, I know. Belinda had a great game."

I decided to play it cool and keep to basketball for a while, but I hoped she might bring up taking me to the cemetery. "And I guess Jessie predicted it. They're three and oh, now."

"Yeah, they're on a roll."

"Kaiser?"

"What?" Rebecca smiled at me but looked perplexed at the same time.

"'They're on a *roll*,'" I quoted. "Kaiser roll?" I grinned and waited.

She laughed and shot me a look that said, 'You're so silly,' which melted

97

my insides to goo.

I laughed with her for a minute and then said, "I was able to get the results of the tournament into the winter sports preview."

"Oh, yeah?" She sounded surprised.

"Yeah. And I didn't dis Jessie or anything."

"Pfft. She'd deserve it," Rebecca muttered under her breath.

I acted as if I didn't hear her and asked, "What'd you say?"

She snorted. "Nothing. Hey, I promised I'd take you out to Greystone. How's Wednesday after school?"

Awesome, awesome, awesome! "Uh, yeah," I said with as much cool as I could come up with, "that'd be great. Thanks." Oh, my God, I was busting at the seams, but I didn't want to scare her away now that I had made an inch of progress. "Should I walk to your house?" I hoped she'd say she'd pick me up because she lived a couple of miles away. I could always go for a run, but then I'd be all sweaty, and I didn't want Rebecca to see me that way.

"Uh, no. I'll pick you up at your house. It'll have to be around 4:00, though, because Ms. Adams wants me to rehearse a piece with the dance troupe beforehand."

Oh, God. Maybe I shouldn't have pushed her into taking me to the cemetery. I had forgotten about her afternoon dance rehearsals, but I smiled inside. She had actually put thought into it and had even talked to her dance teacher about it.

"Okay," I said. "I've got nowhere to be." That wasn't true, actually. I had a girls' swim meet to go to on Wednesday afternoon, but I'd just skip that and head home to get ready. I wish I could go down to the basement dance studio and watch her rehearse, but I didn't want her to think I was some kind of stalker or something.

I smiled at her, tucked my unstarted French worksheet into my notebook, and jammed both into my backpack. Just before the bell rang, I saw Jessie standing outside the classroom door. No surprise there. Rebecca saw her, too, and sighed. And it wasn't a "good to see you" kind of sigh. It was more of a "can't believe I have to deal with you" sigh.

Jessie sneered at me through the small glass window in the door as if she were proud of herself—like she had gotten the better of me or something. As much as I was pleased that Rebecca seemed agitated by Jessie's mere presence, I was also upset because Rebecca seemed upset. But I couldn't hand her the panda bear now. Not in front of Jessie.

Rebecca bolted when the bell rang without even saying goodbye. I stayed in my seat and sighed. If she had any interest in me at all, she would have been friendlier. Yeah, reality hit me hard in the back of Mme Depardieu's classroom at that moment. Rebecca was just being nice to me and honoring the promise she'd made me.

Glumly, I reopened my backpack and dug underneath my books for the somewhat flattened panda bear. And on my way out of the classroom, I mumbled, "What a stupid freakin' idea. It's not gonna happen, Devon." I threw the bear in the trashcan.

~~~

Wednesday afternoon rolled in cold and dreary, but I barely noticed the weather as I sat on the living room couch, coat in hand, trying to stay calm and breathe normally. I don't know why I was so nervous. I guess I just couldn't figure out how to get my feelings for Rebecca to go away. And since I had finally figured out that Rebecca didn't want anything to do with me, I kind of felt bad that I was making her take me to the cemetery that afternoon. It had become so much easier to focus on Grandma now.

She said she'd pick me up at 4:00. At 3:58, I heard a noise outside the house and leaped off the couch to the living room windows. Nope, just an old car passing by. I sat back down and watched the clock some more.

I was glad Dad was still at work and Mom was at the grocery store because I didn't want them to witness my jitters.

I wondered if my mom would pass out over me liking girls. What if I confided in her the way I did with Missy? Maybe she'd take it okay, but I wasn't ready to spill those beans. Not yet. Not before I'd even had a girlfriend. And my dad. I had no idea what his reaction would be. He would probably just follow my mom's lead, so if she were cool about it, he would be, too. If she hit the ceiling, he would, too, and then he'd make me replaster and paint.

I looked at the clock. 4:05. My mind went into a spin. *She forgot. She was only being polite. She didn't really want to bring me to see Grandma.* I checked my cell phone for a text. Nothing. I groaned in misery but then told myself to chill out. It wasn't as if we were on some kind of secret spy mission with synchronized watches or something. Four o'clock at my house could be three fifty-two at hers. Or maybe her dance thing ran over.

I got up and went to the bathroom near the front door. I looked at myself in the mirror. Yeah, I still looked okay. Hoop earrings—check. Hair up—check. Shaved legs—oops, nope, but it was the last day of November. No one was going to see my legs until May, anyway.

Satisfied with the mirror, I went back into the living room to continue my clock-watching vigil. It was 4:10. Missy's advice had been to find a way to be alone with her, and this was the only way I had come up with for now. What if Rebecca was still icy cold to me like she'd been all week? And what were we going to talk about? What if this actually was just a trip to see my grandmother at the cemetery?

When I heard a car pull into the driveway, I practically leaped off the living room couch like Belinda Carmichael, leaping for a rebound. It didn't sound like my mom's car, so I was pretty sure it was Rebecca's. I took a couple of deep breaths to get my heart out of my throat and snuck a peak through the curtains. To my astonishment, a hearse sat idling in the driveway. I laughed as I opened the front door.

I waved to Rebecca as she got out of the driver's side of the hearse. She shrugged and smiled in embarrassment. "Sorry, Devon. Mom needed the other car today, but I figured since we were going to the cemetery anyway, we'd fit right in."

I wasn't sure how I felt about driving around in the black hearse, but if the hearse held Rebecca, then I'd go along with it. "No problem," I said as I opened the passenger-side door and got in. The scent of Rebecca's rose perfume wrapped itself around me and made my insides tremble. I floated into the car on her rose petals and settled softly onto the passenger seat. I took a couple of deep breaths to calm my quickening pulse and clear my head before I closed the door. Being alone with her was going to be way harder than I thought.

I forced myself to focus on the dashboard before I braved looking at her again. The inside of the hearse was surprisingly cozy and looked just like any other car in the front. Of course, all I had to do was turn around to see where the similarities ended. I didn't dare look, afraid of what I might see.

"Ready to go?" Rebecca asked and put the hearse in reverse.

"One question before we go."

"Sure, what is it?"

"Is there a casket in here?"

She burst out laughing, which eased my mind. "No. I'd never do that to you." She backed the car out of my driveway and headed toward Greystone Cemetery. "We don't take the hearse to the food store or anything, but Mom said I could drive it if we just went to the cemetery and back."

I laughed. "No Scoopalicious? I owe you a hot fudge brownie sundae."

"You don't owe me—"

"I know, but I want to buy you one." *And now I'm really sounding like a stalker.* I cringed and held my breath, not sure how she would react.

She laughed, and I exhaled under my breath. She said, "And I'd love for you to buy me ice cream, but maybe we should wait until summer. It's a bit cold right now."

"Yeah, okay. Hey," I said way too sharply, "I've been meaning to ask you something."

"Yeah?"

"Does your family live in the funeral home?"

She laughed again. What an amazing sound. "No, we live in the house next door. Do you remember the brick house to the right of the funeral home as you're looking at it?"

"Vaguely."

She smiled at me and said, "Yeah, you probably had other things on your mind, but that's where we live."

We were stopped at the main traffic light in the middle of town, and I couldn't help but remember that the last time I saw the hearse go through this part of town, we had been able to run all the lights. It was then that the real reason for my trip with Rebecca started to hit me. The light turned green, and we headed through town and out onto Grasse River-Unionville Road.

"Let's see," Rebecca said. "I guess I'll be buying *you* a raspberry ice cream with…Wait, don't tell me." She put her index finger in the air as if to stop me

101

from speaking. "Chocolate sprinkles. Right?"

"Bingo. *Tu as tout bon.*"

"*Tu as tout bon, aussi.*" She smiled and seemed satisfied that she had remembered. I was ecstatic because she had remembered something kind of private about me. Knowing somebody's favorite ice cream was kind of a personal thing.

The road to the cemetery had taken on the browns and grays of winter. My mood changed as we approached the big gates. Rebecca must have sensed my withdrawal because she looked at me and said, "*Tu te sens bien?*"

I swallowed around the lump forming in my throat. "Yeah, I'm okay, but I didn't bring anything. I should have brought flowers or a snow globe."

"A snow globe?"

"Yeah, Grandma collected little glass snow globes. But that would be stupid to bring to a cemetery. I should have brought flowers." The closer we got to Grandma's grave, the more I babbled. I hadn't been back to the cemetery since the day of the funeral. But today, she'd actually be under the ground. I was glad it was a miserably cold and rainy day and that all the nice snow from that morning's flurries had melted.

"You'll be okay, Devon. *Ça va.*"

She pulled the hearse down the side road leading to my grandmother's grave. My grandfather's grave was right next to hers, and I instantly felt bad because I had planned this whole trip to see Grandma. Not once did I think about paying my respects to Grandpa. I steeled myself as I got ready to open the door and decided to rectify my misdeed and include my grandfather in all my thoughts from now on.

I needed to hurry up since darkness fell quickly in a North Country winter. I wanted to get this whole visit thing over with, but when I opened the door, I couldn't move. The heaviness of the damp earth paralyzed me as I stared at the oh-so-obvious new sod over my grandmother's grave. I had been an idiot trying to combine alone time with Rebecca with a trip to see my grandmother. I took a deep breath for strength and got out of the hearse without looking back.

A wooden marker with my grandmother's name, "Mildred B. Raines," identified the grave. Obviously, the headstone hadn't been installed yet. I stood on the sod and then leaped off. I had been standing right on her. I was mortified. I didn't know the right protocol. You always see people in the movies standing in front of the headstone crying or something. How could they? I wasn't sure what to do, so I stood off to the side and looked at the wooden marker. I tried to come up with some kind of prayer, but I couldn't remember any from the couple of times Mom and Dad tried to take Missy and me to the Presbyterian Church on the corner. I don't know why we quit going, but I could have used some good lines right about now. I almost laughed. The journalist was out of words.

I decided to speak to Grandma as if she were right in front of me. "Grandma," I said in a shaky voice, "I'm sorry you had to die. Dad said that everyone has their time, but I wish it weren't your time yet. I'm still in high school, Grandma. I haven't even gone to college yet."

Tears welled up in my eyes, and I felt a little self-conscious, so I snuck a look at Rebecca. She was looking the other way. She had stayed in the hearse, probably to give me some space or something.

"So, anyway, Grandma. Missy's still in college, too. She let me have that New York City snow globe that she got you. I hope that was okay. I promise to take good care of it." I shuffled my feet on the grass, not sure what to say next. I blurted out, "Grandma, I'm sorry you had to leave so soon. Are you with Grandpa? Are you happy? Is there a heaven, Grandma? Do you see me?"

If she was looking down at me from heaven, I'm sure she was shaking her head, thinking that I was full of way too many questions or something. I took a deep breath and said, "I hope you're okay with Missy taking back her room. I kind of need my own space these days. See that girl in the hearse? Oh, yeah, sorry about coming here in a hearse again. But Rebecca offered, and, well, here I am. Anyway, that's Rebecca. And…" I wasn't sure how to come out to my grandmother. I decided to go for it because, well, she wouldn't be able to answer me anyway. I sighed. "I like her. I mean, I really like her. You know about me now, right? Now that you're, uh, over there? And Grandpa, does he know? Well, Rebecca's so pretty. And, Grandpa, she likes fishing. Uses worms and all." I nodded my head as if he could see me. "But there's one thing I don't know how to do. I don't know how to tell her that I like her. If you have any ideas, any ideas at all, let me know. Okay?"

I wasn't sure what to say next, so I just told my grandparents that I hoped they were having a good time in heaven but not to expect me up there any time soon. I laughed and wiped at the few remaining tears in my eyes, glad I could present a relatively tear-free face to Rebecca.

I opened the door to the hearse and was shocked to see Rebecca crying in the driver's seat.

"What's wrong?" I asked and slid into the passenger seat.

She didn't answer me. She just shook her head, wiped her eyes, and stared out the windshield. She reached into her coat pocket and pulled out a bundle of tissues. She looked at me, and her voice was heavy when she said, "These were for you, but it looks like I'm the one who needs them." She dabbed at her nose and then looked out the window again.

"Are you okay? Did I do something?" While part of me wondered what I'd done to make her cry, another part tried to wrap itself around the fact that she had brought tissues for me. She had been thinking about me.

She sighed and looked back at me with the saddest eyes I'd ever seen. It was a sadness I couldn't quite describe. I wished I still had the panda bear. That would have made her smile.

"No, Devon, you didn't do anything."

"Okay." I wasn't sure what to do or what to say. We sat in the hearse as the sky darkened.

After forever, she finally said, "I'm just...Oh, I don't know. I'm just not happy with a certain friend of mine. That's all."

I knew instantly. "Jessie?"

She looked at me as if amazed that I had figured out who she was talking about so quickly. "How'd you know?"

"I don't know anything, really. You just seemed, uh, annoyed with her the other day."

"You noticed that?"

"Sorry."

"Oh, don't be sorry." Rebecca flicked her hand as if knocking away something offensive. She looked away. "I'm so done with her."

Done with her? My heart lifted and sang a happy tune, but I squelched my inner rejoicing and said somberly, "What happened?"

She looked toward me as if debating what to say.

I said, "Look, you don't have to share anything. I'm just a stupid nosy journalist."

"No, you're okay. It's not you." She took a deep breath and exhaled—just like she had taught me. "I think you know that Jessie and I were…close."

"I guess."

"And I think you know just how close."

Here it was. Rebecca was coming out to me. Holy tuna on a cracker. She was like me. I squelched my smile but knew my eyes would give me away, so I looked down at my hands in my lap. My brain searched for something to say, and Missy's line came to me. "I wasn't sure." I looked over at her but kept quiet, hoping she'd elaborate.

She searched my face, probably trying to gauge how much information to give me, how much she could trust me.

"Off the record," I said with a cheesy grin.

She laughed, and, as usual, that made me smile even more.

"Okay, deal. Jessie and I have been going out for over a year. Last year, September."

"Oh," was all I could say. I had finally met another person like me, and I was spellbound. Who else was like us? "Is Natalie…you know?"

"No, she's not. She's in love with Jessie's younger brother. That's why she hangs around Jessie so much."

"Did she know about you guys?"

"I think so, but not officially. No one at school knows officially, but it didn't seem to bother Natalie."

I decided that since she had trusted me, I'd reciprocate. "Um, did you know that I was, too?"

She smiled at me, and I was glad she had stopped crying. "Yeah, Devon. I thought maybe you were, but you sort of told me on the power dam field trip when we talked about being *different*." She made air quotes when she said the word different.

"Does Jessie know about me, too?"

Rebecca nodded and said, "Yeah, she had you pegged before I did."

"Oh, God," I said under my breath. On one hand, I was mortified that

Jessie knew, but on the other hand, Rebecca and I had just come out to each other. Oh, the happy dance I wanted to do, but at the cemetery in a hearse just didn't seem like the right place to do it.

"What are you smiling about? Are you happy that Jessie knows?"

"No." I laughed. "No, no, no. I'm just glad that I found some of my people."

This time, Rebecca smiled. "Your *people?*"

"Yeah, I thought I'd be alone for the rest of my life."

"I don't believe that for a second." She looked at me shyly. "You're very attractive, Devon. And I don't think you know that."

I felt my cheeks flush even more. I looked down at my hands again. I'd never thought of myself as *attractive.*

"Oh, now don't go getting all shy on me." She put her hand on my coat sleeve.

I gulped. I couldn't exactly feel her touch on my winter coat, but I got nervous. I felt myself shaking inside. To be alone with Rebecca, to hear her say that she liked girls, and to hear that things were rocky with Jessie—these were the things I had wished for. But now that all of these things had come true, I was scared to death.

She slid her hand down my jacket sleeve and let her hand close over mine. She linked my pinky with hers. "You had a lot of nerve doing this on the bus."

I gulped again. I had trouble swallowing around the lump in my throat. I couldn't say anything. My heart was beating so fast I thought it might leap out of my chest.

She let go of my pinky and grabbed my whole hand again. This was what I wanted, but I still couldn't move. I was paralyzed with fear. Where was my set of brass ones when I needed them?

"Rebecca?"

"Yeah?"

"Jessie's going to kill me if she finds out I'm holding your hand."

"Pfft. No, she's not. I broke up with Jessie after school today. That's why I was late." She let go of my hand and started the engine to the hearse. "C'mon, we'd better go. They're going to lock the gates."

Chapter 11

Flack

The November/December issue of the Gazette had officially been put to bed, and even though we all pleaded to have a free day, Mrs. Gibson cracked the whip, and we got started on the January/February issue. I decided to feature the girls' indoor track team for the next issue of the paper. I had a self-imposed deadline of Friday to get the outline done, which gave me this class period and tomorrow's. The deadline would have been an easy one to make, except for the fact that just yesterday, Rebecca held my hand in the hearse. That always sounded weird to my mental ears, but it was true. And she was the one who had grabbed my hand this time. I frowned as I tried to remember who the coach of the girls' indoor track team was. Ah, how could I concentrate when I couldn't figure out why I had frozen up in the hearse? And, well, being gay was a whole new arena for me, too. With a guy, it was expected that he would do the asking. Like the way Joey took forever to ask out Gail, but he finally did. And the girl was supposed to worry about what she wore while the guy took care of everything else.

I laughed and then muttered under my breath, "Well, that's pretty damn sexist."

"What's pretty damn sexist?" I jumped when I realized that Mike was right behind me.

"You scared the crap out of me. I didn't even hear you slide over."

"I've been calling your name for about three minutes, but you were in space. So I got my passport photo taken and traveled over here to Devonland."

I rolled my eyes. "Sorry. I'm a little preoccupied."

"Understatement."

"Yeah, well, I've just got some things on my mind."

"Me, too. That's why I came over here. I wanted to know how your editing went for the last issue. We didn't get a chance to talk too much, and I have to admit, I expected a lot more questions from you."

I bet you did. "Oh, I got the hang of it pretty fast. With your help and from my sister, I was fine."

"I forgot you could call on Missy. She's still Mrs. Gibson's favorite, you know. She talks about her all the time."

"Yeah, I know. I'm trying to stay out of her shadow."

Mike smiled. "So, the newspaper comes out on Monday. Excited?"

"Terrified."

"I was the same way when my first issue came out in October. I was scared stiff."

"You? I find that hard to believe."

Mike ran a hand through his blonde crew cut and said, "Oh, yeah. And I bet if you ask Missy, she'd tell you she was scared, too, when her first issue came out."

"I hope I survive Monday."

"Hey, listen." He ran a hand through his hair again. "I wanted, uh, I wanted to know if…if it'd be okay if I ate lunch with you guys. With you and Joey and Gail."

His question came straight from outer space. I wasn't sure what to say, but eating lunch with Mike didn't seem like a bad thing. "Yeah, sure. We sit in the corner by the outside doors."

"I know," he said with a twinkle in his eye. "I'll see you at lunch today, okay?"

"Okay." I watched his retreating back and sighed. Gail. It had to be. She was the one who wanted me to ask him out a couple of weeks ago. I guess when I didn't act on her command, she took things into her own hands. Too bad she had no clue that I was of another persuasion. The gay persuasion. I looked back at my computer screen and decided that even though it might not go well with me being a *lezzie* and all, I had to tell Gail sooner rather than later so she wouldn't try to fix me up with any more guys.

I wasn't sure what was going to be hardest—getting Mike to back off, coming out to Gail, or asking Rebecca to go out with me. I guess somewhere in my mind, I decided to unfreeze myself and find the nerve to ask Rebecca out. I had to try, or I'd never know. Maybe I could ask her to go downtown to the Grasse River Christmas tree lighting ceremony tomorrow. No pressure, just hot chocolate, Christmas carols, and, oh yeah, cold. Maybe she would hold my hand again so I could warm her up.

I decided that asking Rebecca out was definitely going to be the hardest of the three.

~~~

I usually got to the cafeteria before Gail and Joey because I came from English right down the hall, but Mr. Hurley, my English teacher, kept us after the bell, so I was later than usual. Rebecca would be in the cafeteria, too, and it would be the first time I'd see her after she held my hand in the hearse. I wasn't sure if I'd get to talk to her, though, since she didn't text me at all last night.

I almost dropped my backpack when I saw Mike sitting at our usual table with Gail and Joey. I had forgotten about him. When Gail saw me, she stood up and waved frantically. If I'd had any doubts about her trying to fix me up with Mike, they were gone now. I waved back and weaved my way through the quickly filling cafeteria.

I plopped my backpack on the table at my usual seat and said, "Hey, guys. Hey, Mike."

"Hey, Devon." Mike half stood up as I sat down across the table from him.

Oh, God. Mike was trying way too hard. How in the world was I going to tell him that I wasn't interested? And it wasn't because of him. How could I let him know that I just wasn't into guys?

I unzipped my backpack and pulled out the turkey wrap with sprouts I had made at home that morning. I decided to start bringing my lunch to school so I could save my allowance for Christmas presents. I wasn't sure yet what I wanted to get for Rebecca; maybe some of that rose perfume she wore that drove me crazy. It was probably way too expensive, but I didn't care.

Gail pulled her sandwich out from her bag.

"Wow," I said impressed. "Roast beef?"

"Yeah, Mom went shopping." She took a big bite. "It's good," she said with her mouth full.

Joey and I laughed, and when we laughed, so did Mike.

Joey said, "Very attractive, honey. Very attractive."

Gail swallowed. "I know. Classy, ain't I?" She made a face at me and then held my gaze a little longer than usual. I knew what she was trying to say. I just let my eyes grow wide so she would know that I understood why Mike was sitting at our table. Best friends have a way of being psychic with each other. It was too bad that her psychic abilities stopped just short of knowing I was into girls.

Gail smiled back and then turned to Mike. "So, Mike, what are your hobbies?"

What are your hobbies? Oh, c'mon, Gail. I couldn't believe how much she pushed sometimes.

Mike said, "Oh, well, I run cross-country and—"

He didn't have a chance to finish because Gail butted in. "No kidding. Devon runs all the time."

He turned to me with wide eyes. "You do? I didn't know that. You're not on cross-country or track, are you?"

I looked at his blonde crew cut and his blue eyes and thought that he really was kind of good-looking. "No, no. I just run for health, I guess. Running clears your head, you know?"

He smiled in such a way that made me cringe. He thought we were connecting, bonding, hitting it off. I had to stop this whole thing before it got too far along. I didn't want to get stuck in this already awkward situation.

Joey picked up the thread of the conversation and talked about how he got in the zone when he worked out in the weight room. I took the opportunity to look down four tables and see if I could catch a glimpse of Rebecca. I saw her usual set of friends, including the guys at the basketball game, but she wasn't at the table. But, unfortunately, I caught Jessie's evil scowl.

"What?" I said when Gail tapped me on the arm.

"I said we're going to the tree lighting tomorrow night. Do you want to go?"

"Yeah," I said too quickly. I realized too late that Gail wanted me to go with them, and *them* included Mike. My plan to ask Rebecca to go with me to the tree lighting had just gone up in smoke.

"Excellent," Gail said. "Joey and I will pick you guys up."

I choked down the rest of my turkey wrap as Gail and Joey discussed the arrangements with Mike and me. I nodded a couple of times, but what I was actually doing was searching the cafeteria for Rebecca, table by table by table. It made perfect sense, I realized, that she wouldn't be sitting with Jessie. They had broken up, after all, so Rebecca probably sat somewhere else. I couldn't remember another group of Black kids in the cafeteria, and then I felt weird about my assumption that Rebecca would only sit with Black kids. I stamped my foot in frustration when I couldn't find her anywhere.

The conversation at my table turned to college and who our guidance counselors would be when we were seniors. I continued my covert search for Rebecca, but when she didn't turn up, I tried to find her with telepathy. That didn't work either, and my inattentiveness earned me a kick from Gail under the table.

I smiled back at Mike. Yeah, Gail had set the whole thing up, all right. And now Mike and I had a date. But, then again, it wasn't exactly a date since we were going in a group. And since we were going in a group, maybe I could still ask Rebecca to go with us. It was a bad idea, I knew, but I was desperate.

~~~

Although lunch had been stressful, French was pretty routine, except for the fact that Rebecca sat stonily next to me. Okay, that made it kind of stressful, too, but I hadn't yet figured out how to break her mood. She had been late to class, and we still hadn't had a chance to talk to each other since she dropped me off at home after the cemetery yesterday. I didn't want to be too pushy, so I didn't text or call her last night.

We were supposed to be working on yet another worksheet, but I decided to take a chance and talk to her. "Rebecca?" She looked up at me. "Are you okay?"

She simply nodded but then went back to her worksheet.

I tried again. "Thanks for driving me to Greystone."

She looked back at me and smiled politely. "No problem."

111

"I'm sorry about your, you know, with Jessie. That can't be fun." *And why am I bringing this up in French class with all these people around? Why am I bringing it up at all? I'm an idiot. A desperate idiot.*

"Oh, well, you know how it is."

"Actually, I don't."

"No? You've never broken up with someone?"

"I've never gone out with anyone." *And why did I just admit that?* I cringed at my too-honest self.

"Devon, I find that hard to believe."

So, go out with me and change that. I felt my cheeks get hot, but I ignored my embarrassment because at least she was talking to me. I had to savor every moment.

"Listen. It was long overdue, I have to tell you."

"I'm sorry things didn't work out." I tried to keep the glee out of my voice, but I'm pretty sure she heard.

Rebecca had been attempting to do her worksheet while we talked, but she put her pen down and sighed. She looked at me for a long time as if wondering whether or not she could trust me. Finally, she leaned in closer and whispered, "I got tired of everything being all about her. I couldn't have any other friends. I couldn't walk to my own locker by myself at the end of the day. And I got tired of doing everything she wanted to do. I never got to see any movies that I wanted to see. We always went to some kind of shoot-em-up movie. Never a chick flick like I wanted. We always talked about her basketball games and practices, but she never asked me how my dance routines were coming along. I doubt she even knows the date of my dance concert."

"December 18th," I said before I could stop myself.

"See?" She pointed at me. "She wouldn't know that."

I seemed to have opened up the floodgates because Rebecca went on and on about Jessie's selfishness. She didn't even stop venting when the bell rang to end class. We packed up our books, and I did an internal happy dance when I saw that Jessie wasn't at the door. Even though Rebecca said she didn't like the fact that Jessie escorted her after French class every day, I was doing the exact same thing. Actually, I had no choice because Rebecca kept talking about Jessie, and it would have been rude to just leave her. As if I even wanted to.

112

On the outside, I wore my best sympathetic face, but on the inside, my stomach did joyful somersaults. She hated Jessie, and that left the door wide open for me. Didn't it?

I knew I was getting way ahead of myself, but the first thing we'd do after the tree lighting ceremony would be to go to the chick flick of her choice. I wouldn't even care how sappy it was. Then we'd talk about her dancing until our voices were sore. But we wouldn't talk about basketball or Jessie. Ever.

When we got to her locker, she laughed. "Oh, my God, Devon. I'm sorry. I've talked your ear off." She touched the sleeve of my shirt. "Thanks for being a good sport about all of this stupidness."

"No problem. I haven't done anything, though."

"Well, you listened. No one's listened to a word I've said in over a year."

"Well, I've got two good ears." I pulled on both my earlobes and then instantly regretted my corniness. She turned from me to work the combination on her locker. I dug down deep to my toes and said, "Hey, Rebecca?"

"Yeah?" She squatted down in front of her locker to put some books away.

"Um, the tree lighting ceremony is tomorrow night downtown. At the firehouse. Do you, maybe, want to go with me?" Oh, God, why did I have to make it sound so much like I was asking her out on a date? Why couldn't I have said something more like, 'Hey, Rebecca, want to check out the tree lighting thing tomorrow night?' That would have been so much better, but I had already cast out my line and was committed.

She was quiet for so long that my jaw started to ache since I was clenching my teeth so hard. I thought maybe she hadn't heard me. "Rebecca?"

"Yeah, I heard you, Devon. I, uh…" She paused for a moment and then looked at me. "Look, you're sweet, but I can't."

A dagger thrust into my heart. I looked around the hallway to make sure no one was within earshot and whimpered, "Don't you like me? At least a little?" God, I was pathetic.

"Oh, Devon. You're amazing. But just forget about me. Okay?"

As if. Maybe it was too soon after Jessie. Maybe I wasn't good-looking enough. Maybe I was too much of a journalism nerd. I know she wanted to leave it at that, but she told me, just the day before, that she found me attractive. I clung to it like a life preserver and tried not to sound defeated

113

when I said, "I can't."

She closed her locker so hard that I jumped at the force of it. She looked me in the eye and said, "Look, if Jessie—"

"If Jessie, what? I thought you guys broke up." I whispered this, but I'm sure she heard the desperation in my voice.

She sighed and looked down quickly. "We *did* break up. And I need to deal with that right now. I can't…" She didn't look at me for the longest time. When she picked her head up, her hard expression forced me to take an involuntary step back.

She said, "Okay, here's the deal. One of my friends called me an Aunt Jemima for hanging out with you."

I know my mouth dropped open, but I couldn't close it. What did that mean? *Aunt Jemima*? That can't be good.

"I'm sorry, Devon," she continued. "You're cool, but I just…can't."

"Why? What's wrong with me?" It felt like someone was twisting my stomach into knots.

Her face softened. "Nothing. There's nothing wrong with you. You're one of the sweetest people I know. It's obvious how much you cared for your grandmother. And you're smart and funny and cute." She said the word 'cute' kind of shyly. "It's, uh…Well, they're saying that I'm not staying in the community. Well, this one guy did. And being called Aunt Jemima means they think I'm acting subservient to whites. They call my Dad Uncle Tom sometimes, but most of this town is white. And white people die, and when you run a funeral home, you serve white people." She swallowed hard, obviously emotional. "I'm sorry. I mean absolutely no disrespect for your grandmother or your family. But, look, I'm already condemned for liking girls, even though I've never come out to anyone formally. I can just tell that a lot of the guys think they can convert me back or something. Idiots." She rolled her eyes. "Oh, Devon, I just can't go out with a white girl right now. It's too much. I like you a whole lot, actually." She looked down again, and I thought for a second that she was going to change her mind. Then, she said firmly, "But I can't." She looked past me down the hallway and said, "I've got to get to my dance rehearsal. I'm sorry."

I stared after her, retreating back. I couldn't believe what I had just heard.

She couldn't go out with me because I was white. Even though she said it herself, she thought I was cute, smart, and funny. She couldn't go out with me because my skin wasn't as dark as hers, and I wasn't part of the Black community. It was true, though. I hadn't made any effort to make a single Black friend before now. I think I finally had a glimpse of what the word discrimination meant.

I didn't have time to fall into a depression because as soon as Rebecca turned the corner, Jessie appeared from out of nowhere. I jumped and fell back against Rebecca's locker.

"What do you—" I started to ask.

Jessie didn't let me finish. She poked my shoulder with her rock-hard finger and growled, "If I ever catch you alone again, Raines, you'd better make peace with God, 'cuz you're gonna need Him when I get through with you."

Her hot breath in my face made me grimace. And even though I was shaking from head to toe, I asked, "Why do you hate me so much? I haven't done anything to you."

Jessie's steel-hardened glare softened for a micro-second, but then her face stiffened again. "As if," she said slowly, "you didn't know. All she ever talks about is you. All the time." She slammed her open palm against the locker right next to my head. The sound of metal denting so close to my ear made me whimper, which I'm sure she thoroughly enjoyed. When I tried to move away, she put her other arm up, blocking my escape. She looked me right in the eye, and I swallowed hard. I'd never been in a fight before, and I didn't know what to do.

"Just stay away from Rebecca." She stepped back but poked me in the shoulder with so much fury that I wanted to crawl into the locker digging into my back. I tried to slow my pounding heart as she stormed down the hallway.

Chapter 12

Phew

Mrs. Gibson pounded the keys on her keyboard so loudly that I couldn't concentrate. I wasn't happy hanging around with Mrs. Gibson after school on a Friday, but I was doing my best to avoid Jessie. If I hung out at school long enough, maybe she'd get tired of waiting to beat me up. Of course, I didn't know for sure if she was actually stalking me or not, but I didn't want to take that chance.

I doubled my efforts to focus on the email in front of me. Julia Knight, one of the girls' sports reporters from the sophomore class, submitted an article proposal to me about the history of girls' sports at Grasse River High School. I'd gotten the email from Julia on Wednesday but hadn't had a chance to get back to her until now.

Wednesday. Yeah, Wednesday had been the good day. That was the day three amazing things had happened. Rebecca broke up with Jessie, she told me she was gay, and she held my hand. Three amazing things in my favor. But Thursday—yesterday—that was the day that sucked. It sucked for two reasons. First, Rebecca turned me down flat when I asked her out. She was the first person I had ever asked out in my life, and I got rejected. Slammed down. Dismissed. All because I was white. Well, maybe there was more to it than that. Maybe she liked someone else. That would have been easier to stomach than the fact that she didn't want to go out with me on account of my pale skin. Or maybe she just didn't like me. But I couldn't bring myself to believe that. And the second reason Thursday sucked was because Jessie Crowler almost beat the crap out of me. And that's why I was hiding in the journalism room with Mrs. Gibson on a Friday afternoon. Of course, I was getting major suck-up points from Mrs. Gibson, but I really didn't care about that at all.

Rebecca wasn't in the cafeteria at lunch again, and in French she didn't talk to me either. Well, to be fair, I was the one doing most of the non-talking. All I kept thinking about was how white I was and wondering how I could work on my tan because maybe she'd go out with me if I wasn't so glary white. But getting a tan in December this far north was impossible. Sunlight was a luxury we couldn't seem to afford in the North Country, especially during the winter. God, like my dad, was probably trying to save on the galactic power bill or something. But, c'mon, the shade of my skin wasn't really the issue. My ethnicity, my heritage, my background. Those were the issues.

But right now, I needed to get my head back into Julia's proposal and finish up so I could literally run home. She proposed an article about how the Title IX initiative from so long ago changed girls' sports at Grasse River High School. Title IX was supposed to equalize boys' and girls' educations in public schools, including sports. It seemed Julia's mom played softball at Grasse River in the seventies before Title IX went into effect. Julia said her mom's team was bussed to one of the local elementary schools, where they played on a neglected field with a rusty weed-infested backstop. And the grass was never cut, she said. The boys' baseball team, on the other hand, played on a beautifully manicured field right on the school's property. The photos Julia attached were incredible. The difference between the miserable girls' field and the meticulously groomed boys' field was an absolute crime. Did people have their heads buried in the sand back then, or what? What a shame it took a federal law to make things more equal.

The more girls' games I went to in my role as sports editor, the more I realized that sports were way addicting. I understood more and more why it sucked for girls to get the shaft in terms of crappy fields or bad equipment. I loved Julia's story idea, but she needed to flesh it out a bit more to show how Title IX influenced other girls' sports like basketball and field hockey. And the January/February issue might be too soon. The February/March issue would be too crowded with winter sports wrap-ups and spring sports previews. The best issue for Julia's Title IX article would be April/May. I felt odd making such a huge decision about what went into the newspaper, but Mike told me that editors made decisions like that all the time. I wrote back to Julia telling her what a great idea her article was and included a few suggestions. I ran the spell checker and then sent it off. I saved both her proposal and my email response in my editor's folder.

Mike was the one who suggested I save all of my email responses. He said it would save me time later because I could look up what I'd said to whom and when. He was smart. I was glad I could learn from him. I closed up my files and turned off the computer. I got ready to run home, backpack and all so that I wouldn't get beaten up by a psycho basketball player, and if I actually did make it home, I had to figure out a way to break up with Mike at the tree lighting ceremony tonight, even though we weren't actually seeing each other.

~~~

My mom called up the stairs to me. "Devon, I think Gail and Joey are here."

"Okay," I called down. I checked myself in the mirror. Regular gold posts, hair down, nothing that screamed as if I'd made an effort. I flicked off the light in my room and headed down the hallway. I paused in front of my grandmother's room and said, "Wish me luck, Grandma. I've got to break up with someone before I've even gone out with him."

I took the steps two at a time.

My mom looked up from her book. "Have fun."

My dad muted the sitcom blaring from the TV and said, "Be back by midnight."

"Okay, Dad. See you later." I snatched my coat out of the closet, threw it on, and headed out the door.

I'd be home well before midnight if I could help it. I waved at Gail and hopped in the backseat behind her. "When did it get so cold? Why are we doing this?"

Gail turned around and said, "Tradition. That's why. And you know as well as I do, dork, that it's an excuse to get out of the house."

"Yeah, I guess."

Joey backed the car out of the driveway and headed in the opposite direction of the firehouse where the tree-lighting ceremony was held.

I said, "Hey, where are we going?"

Joey laughed, and Gail said, "Did you forget so soon? We have to pick up Mike."

How could I forget? "Oh, yeah. I guess I don't know where he lives."

"And now you will," Gail said with finality.

Gail chatted away in the front seat about the latest gossip going around school involving one of the cheerleaders and her boyfriend. The shop teacher, it seemed, caught them smoking pot in her car. I was completely uninterested but threw in a couple of well-placed "mm-hmm's" and "oh, really's" so she'd think I was listening.

We pulled up the long driveway to an old farmhouse. I couldn't tell in the dark, but I didn't think Mike's family worked a farm. Lots of people in the North Country lived in old farmhouses but weren't into farming.

Mike bounded out his front door with a wide-open red plaid hunter's jacket and a hunter's cap, the kind with the ear flaps. Even if I were straight, there would be no frickin' way I'd go out with Mike if he were a hunter. And I think my grandmother would have been more upset about me going out with a hunter than she would with me going out with a girl. But what would Grandma feel about me going out with a girl who was Black? Grandma was from another generation, but maybe she would have been enlightened enough to see past prejudice and ignorance. Yes, that's what it was. Ignorance. Basic, unadulterated ignorance.

"Hey, Devon. How are ya?" A blast of cold air came in with Mike as he climbed into the backseat with me.

"Look's like you're going hunting." Nothing like getting that right out into the open.

"Oh, yeah. But I'm not a hunter." He leaned in closer to me and whispered, "I just like the look."

"Hey," Gail barked from the front seat. "What are you two doing back there?"

Oh, please. She really is loving this too much. "Oh, keep a lid on it, Marsters." I nudged her shoulder from the back seat.

"Well," she said with fake indignation. "Be that way, Raines."

"Catfight," Joey hollered.

"Whoo hoo," Mike joined in.

Gail meowed, which made the two guys howl even louder.

"Hey," I yelled. "Get yourselves together. We've got a tree to light."

Mike laughed. "Who's got the lighter?"

"I've got some matches," Gail said.

"No, no. I've got it," Joey said. "We stop at Stewart's, buy a gas can, fill it up, pour it all over the tree, and *then* Gail can throw her matches on it."

"Yeah," Mike said. "This'll be the best tree lighting ceremony ever."

I shook my head in disbelief. "You are all c-r-a-z-y. Certifiable, I think." Even though I acted as if my friends were out of their minds, I liked hanging out with them. And, I had to admit, Mike fit right in with us dorks. I felt doubly sorry that I had to be cold to him tonight.

Gail pointed at the crowd gathering in front of the firehouse. "Look how many people are here already. We're never going to find a parking spot."

A church choir was singing from the platform. I checked my watch. "Hey, we still have twenty minutes. Plenty of time."

"Cool," Joey said. "I'm going to go around the block and see if we can park at the Big M."

Joey found an open spot in a dark corner near the supermarket's receiving platform. We parked and then walked back around the block toward the firehouse. We made believe we were smoking as our breath vaporized in the crisp night air. The tree lighting ceremony was kind of dumb, but here we were with everybody else who lived in Grasse River. And as we fought through the throng of people, I had to laugh because, once again, I was relegated to second-class status. Joey and Gail held hands as they carved a path through the people while Mike and I tagged along behind. I hoped that Mike wasn't trying to figure out a way to hold my hand. Just in case, I kept my hands jammed deep into my coat pockets.

We found a not-too-crowded spot by the nativity scene. We stood around for a moment when Mike blurted, "Hey, do you girls want hot chocolate? I think they have some at the firehouse."

"Sure," I said and nodded my head. "Thanks."

Mike smiled. I got the feeling that he thought he had just scored a point with me. Well, he had kind of, but in a friendship way. I'm sure that wasn't the kind of point he wanted it to be, though.

"Cool, we'll be right back." He tapped Joey on the arm, and the two guys took off toward the firehouse.

I stepped in next to Gail and rubbed shoulders with her. "Why is it so cold?"

"Because it's December, dork. But Joey keeps me warm."

I almost laughed out loud at her unspoken hint. "Gail…" I stopped because I wasn't sure how to tell her that I wasn't interested in Mike that way.

"What? You sound so serious all of a sudden."

"I just…It's Mike. I know you're pushing for me to go out with him."

"Me?" She put a hand to her chest as if to deny her involvement in any such thing.

"Yeah, you, dorkhead. I just don't like him like that."

"Oh, c'mon, Devon." She looked at me as if I had two heads. "What's not to like? He's cute, he's smart, and he's into the newspaper as much as you are. He's a runner, too, just like you."

"Yeah, yeah. All those things. And I do like him. I just don't like him like that."

Gail sighed and nodded toward the guys heading toward us, holding two Styrofoam cups of hot chocolate each. "Don't make such a fast decision. Why don't you wait until after the tree lighting and after we spend time alone with the guys at Bruster?"

"Oh, no you don't. I'm not going to Bruster with him." I didn't say my next thoughts out loud but stared at her wide-eyed and screamed in my head, '*You and Joey are going to make out in the front seat, and Mike and I'll be uncomfortable, but then he might try something. So, no frickin' way am I going on a double date, or whatever you call it, with you and Joey.*' I didn't say any of it, but I did think it—loudly.

"Oh, c'mon, Dev. What do you have to lose? He's a great guy."

I knew she wasn't going to let up, and the guys were almost on us.

"Hey, just drop it. Okay? Can we talk? Tomorrow?" I had to tell her about me, and I had to do it soon because I couldn't take the pressure anymore.

"Oh, but me and Joey are—"

"Can't you guys be apart for two minutes? God." Maybe it was the pressure of the guys approaching, but I couldn't help my mini-explosion. I felt bad instantly, but it was already out there, and I couldn't take it back.

She looked at me for a long time, long enough for Mike and Joey to reach us. Mike handed me my hot chocolate, and Joey handed Gail hers.

I thanked Mike and took a sip. I wished the hot chocolate was actually hot because my outburst at Gail turned an already cold evening colder.

"Hey, honey," Gail grabbed her boyfriend's arm. "I hope you're not disappointed, but me and Devon want to go to the mall tomorrow afternoon. We've got some Christmas shopping to do. Can we go to the movies another time?" She gave him her best boo-boo face.

I could tell that he couldn't resist her. She had him wrapped around her little finger. "Sure," he said. "No problem. I wear a size large and prefer my jewelry gold."

"Ha, ha," Gail said with exaggerated mirth. "But don't worry, honey, I've already got something special planned for you."

I looked at Mike and grimaced. He rolled his eyes in agreement.

Inside, I thanked Gail for not getting too upset by my outburst. She must have had her sixth sense radar going and understood that I needed my best friend.

The Grasse River fire chief got everyone's attention when the microphone squealed us into covering our ears. As the chief began introducing the various Grasse River dignitaries on stage, I felt Mike shuffle toward me until our arms touched. I wasn't sure how to move away without making him uncomfortable, but, hey, I was already uncomfortable, so I broke contact and moved closer to Gail. I think he took the hint because he didn't try to move closer again.

After what seemed like two hours of speeches, I looked at my watch. The actual lighting of the tree was way overdue. I shook my head I wanted to get this stupid Christmas tree lit and then go home.

"What?" Mike asked me.

He asked it so quickly that he must have been watching my every move. Kind of the way I did with Rebecca. It was not a good feeling. I made a mental note to stop stalking Rebecca. She told me to forget about her anyway, so maybe I would. Maybe I really was going to be alone for the rest of my life.

Mike was still looking at me. I said, "Oh, uh, I was just thinking that these things never start on time."

"Yeah," he said and held my gaze.

I looked away quickly. *There will be no eye gazing, young man*, I thought to myself and hoped he heard me.

The chief started the countdown to the tree lighting, and Gail smiled at me. She must have witnessed my awkward exchange with Mike. I smiled back and was glad she and I were still okay. At least, I hoped we were still okay. I wondered what she'd do when I came out to her at the mall tomorrow.

~~~

My mom pulled the car up to the main entrance of the Maplewoods Mall. "What time should I pick you girls up?"

I took off my seatbelt and looked at Gail as if consulting her mentally. I said, "Uh, well, it's eleven now, so maybe three?" Gail nodded.

"Okay, you girls have a good time and be safe."

"Okay, Mom. Thanks." I got out of the car and met Gail on the sidewalk.

Gail had been smooth last night about getting Joey to drop Mike off first and then me right after the ceremony. I'm sure Mike was confused about the shortened evening, but Gail just acted as if that was all we had planned to do. And now I had four hours to figure out a way to come out to her. I called Missy earlier that morning for a consultation, but she advised me against telling Gail. I thought about it all morning but decided to go against my big sister's advice. Missy said I might lose my best friend. I prayed that Missy was wrong, for once.

"Hey," Gail said, "let's hit the toy store. I want to get Joey a sports car. He wants a real one, but a toy one'll have to do this time."

"Sure." I unzipped my coat and stuffed my gloves in one pocket and my scarf in the other. I always felt like an Eskimo in the stores during the winter.

We reached the toy store, and Gail headed off to the toy car section. I wandered around and found myself in front of a shelf filled with stuffed animals. The display made me think of the black and white panda bear I had thrown in the trash at school. A devious plan sprang to mind. Rebecca told me to forget about her, but I was too far gone for that. If I had the nerve, I'd begin the implementation of my devious plan on Monday, probably in French class. I sifted through the miniature stuffed animals and picked out a penguin, a Dalmatian, a whale, a cow, a zebra, and a skunk—although I'm not so sure the skunk was a good idea. And best of all, I even found another panda bear.

"You've got a boatload," Gail said as she watched me dump the stuffed animals on the checkout counter. She had a bag in her hand so she must have found the sports car she'd been searching for.

"Yeah, I got lucky." I didn't elaborate, but I was ready to lie if she asked. I was going to say that they were for Missy's dorm room and that Missy had a black and white comforter or something.

All the stores in the mall were jammed with Christmas stuff. Each store blasted its own Christmas music and all the songs mixing together was kind of annoying. I think the cacophony of sounds added to my thundering mental clock ticking down on freaking out my best friend.

A group of French-speaking Canadians walked by us. Gail nudged me in the arm. "Half of Canada is here, eh?"

"Shut up, eh?" I giggled. Ah, this was the Gail I knew. I breathed a sigh of relief. Maybe this wouldn't be so hard after all.

We passed by the jewelry cart where I bought those earrings with Rebecca exactly three weeks earlier. The same saleswoman stood at the cart. An overwhelming sense of nostalgia overtook me. Nostalgia for that brief moment I shared with Rebecca. She had made me feel special that day.

The saleswoman must have sensed me staring in her direction because she looked up from her customer, smiled, and said, "Merry Christmas."

"Oh, Merry Christmas." My heart started pounding. Did the saleswoman know? How could she?

"Who was that?" Gail asked as we walked on.

"Oh, I don't know. I bought earrings there a few weeks ago. Maybe she remembered me."

"Weird."

"Yeah," I agreed.

Gail wanted to look at the next cart, but my heart almost stopped. Glass snow globes filled the shelves. They were the same kind of snow globes that my grandmother collected. Used to collect. I picked up the closest one and shook it. The snow drifted around tiny pine trees and two tiny deer. My grandmother would have loved this one. She loved the Adirondack Mountains. I felt my chest tighten and my heart grow heavy. I shook the snow globe again, mesmerized by the falling plastic flakes. Tears were in my eyes before I could stop them, and the falling snow became a blizzard in my blurred vision. I squeezed my eyes shut, hoping I wouldn't break down sobbing in the mall. A knot grew in my throat, and despite my best efforts, a stream of tears started falling down my cheeks. I felt a protective arm go around me, and it startled me to open my eyes.

"Are you okay?" Gail asked.

I started to nod, but the look of compassion in her eyes sent me over the brink. I shook my head, "No," and buried my face in her shoulder and cried. I couldn't help it, and I didn't care if anyone saw me.

When I caught my breath, Gail said, "C'mon. Let's go over here." She took the snow globe from me and put it back on the cart before shuffling me to a blessedly empty bench. I used the sleeve of my jacket to wipe at my tears.

"Sorry," I said and attempted a laugh.

"It's okay, Dev. What happened?"

I took a deep breath and held it. When I was sure I wouldn't start crying again, I exhaled. "Grandma collected those." Tears welled up in my eyes again as I pointed to the cart.

"Oh, I'm so sorry. This must be so hard for you. Christmas and all." She patted my hand in consolation.

"Yeah."

"Hey, you know what?" Gail got perky.

"What?"

"You know what always makes me feel better?"

"What?"

"Ice cream."

I laughed and let myself be led to the busy food court. Instead of ice cream, we decided on lunch instead and settled on the wrap place. After we got our food, we claimed a table from a couple of senior citizens who were just getting up. I took the paper off my turkey wrap and took a bite. I hadn't had breakfast, so I was hungry, especially since I'd gone for a run that morning in the frigid temperature after calling Missy. I had been trying to clear my head, but the bitter cold made my lungs burn, so I only went out about a mile.

Gail opened her roast beef wrap. "Okay, so you dragged me out here to the busiest mall in the free world. What is going on with you?"

My stomach tied itself up in knots, and I pushed my wrap off to one side. I thought I was ready for this. God, maybe Missy was right, maybe I shouldn't tell Gail yet.

Gail pushed on. "Do you have big news or something? Or maybe you just missed me." She batted her eyelashes and smiled, but the curiosity was plain on her face.

I took a sip of my green iced tea. I kind of felt like throwing up, actually, but Gail had already witnessed enough of my bodily fluids for one day, so I took another deep breath and decided to get it over with. Missy told me once that I had a set of brass ones. Darned if I could find them now.

My face grew hotter as the silence grew longer.

Gail obviously couldn't stand my reticence anymore. "Dev, you're killing me here. What is it?"

I felt my blush creep down my neck. Gail must have seen it because she said, "What? Did you murder someone?" She attempted a laugh, but it was unconvincing.

I faked a laugh and said, "No, dork. I just have to tell you something that's really hard for me." I looked around to see if anyone was listening.

Gail looked around, too, and leaned in closer. She whispered, "What is it? You're scaring me."

My stomach clenched again, and I heard myself whisper, "I think I'm gay."

Gail's eyes grew wide. "Gay? A lesbian?" she said way too loudly. "How do you know you're gay? I mean, you've never, like, been with a … girl, right?" She hesitated when she said the word *girl*.

"No, but I don't know. I mean, you knew you liked guys before you were with Joey, right?"

It was Gail's turn to blush. "Okay, okay. Fair point." She took a sip from her iced tea bottle. "Did you just figure this out?"

"No."

"When?"

126

"Seventh grade."

Gail's eyes grew wide. I could see her absorbing the information. She didn't say anything for so long that I thought maybe I truly freaked her out. I mean, I was this big *lezzie* and all, sitting right next to her at the mall.

"Gail?" My voice sounded loud as I broke the increasing silence.

"I've known you for eight years, so you've been gay half that time?"

"I guess so." I laughed, but my insides still trembled. I hoped Gail didn't see how much my hands were shaking as I took a sip of tea.

"Why didn't you tell me before?"

I just shrugged my shoulders.

She gasped. "Oh, my God. Mike!" She dropped her sandwich as if it bit her. "Oh, how awkward. I'm so sorry I did that to you."

"I know. I didn't know how to deal with the whole Mike thing myself. That's why I had to tell you today. Aaah," I faked a scream. "I can't stand the pressure."

"That's why you didn't want to go to Bruster. And I pushed you two together. Eeks, I'm sorry."

"That's okay, but I've got to figure out a way to make Mike go away without revealing my secret. You know?"

"Yeah. And the sooner, the better." She held her sandwich out toward me. "Switch?"

I took her roast beef wrap and asked, "Why do we do this?"

"Because we've been friends forever, and you should have told me sooner."

"Yeah," I smiled at her and hoped we could still be best friends. "Are you okay with, you know, me?"

"Yeah, dork. It's just going to take some getting used to. That's all. Just tell me one thing."

"Okay." The glint in her eye relaxed me a little.

"Did you ever have a crush on me?"

"No!" I said quickly.

"Phew."

"Hey! Why *phew*?"

"Oh, I didn't mean anything by that." She tried unsuccessfully to suppress an embarrassed grin.

"Hey, and don't tell Joey."

Gail didn't say anything. She'd probably been deciding how she was going to break my news to Joey.

I said, "Not yet. Okay?"

"Oh, okay, fine. Spoil my big news. But you're right. I'll just tell him you needed consoling about your grandma with Christmas coming. Which you kind of did, right?"

"Yeah, I guess so."

We clinked sandwiches in salute.

"Hey," she said, pointing to a blonde shopper walking by. "Is she cute?"

"I don't know," I said, surprised by her question. "What am I some kind of expert now?"

"C'mon, help me out. I'm trying to figure out your type."

I laughed and thought about Rebecca and her beautiful dark brown skin. Gail wouldn't figure that one out in a million years. "I don't have a type."

"Everyone has a type."

"Yeah, well, I don't know what that is yet, okay?"

"Am I pretty?" Gail looked at me with completely fabricated innocence in her eyes.

"Yes, you are, but I'm not attracted to you. Okay?"

"Okay, okay. Just asking."

"How about her? She has a nice butt." Gail nodded toward a girl walking by, probably a college student.

"Cut it out, dork. Don't make me regret telling you." I rolled my eyes for her benefit, but inside, I was saying my own *Phew* in relief.

Chapter 13
Operation Black-and-White

Mrs. Gibson's voice at Monday morning's staff meeting barely penetrated the thousand other thoughts running through my head. I snuck a peek at Mike. He grinned from ear to ear when he saw me look at him. I refocused on Mrs. Gibson as I felt my face flush. Obviously, Mike still had ideas about me. About us. This was going to be a long Monday.

Mrs. Gibson dismissed us to our assigned tasks, and I powered up my computer. Out of the corner of my eye, I watched Mike turn his on as well. The computer stations were aligned in a U-shape around the room, and he usually kept his back to me, but that very morning, he turned his computer slightly—probably so he could see me better, I guess. And just as I was thinking this, he turned his head to look in my direction. I had to stop this. Today.

The November/December issue had been handed out that very morning during first-period classes, and I guess I'd find out how well I did as an editor once people read the sports section. But I didn't have time for doubts since I had to get the winter sports articles figured out for the January/February issue. I had allocated space for girls' basketball, cheerleading, indoor track, and swimming. I also saved space for the girls' rifle team, but after going to what I thought was a girls' match recently, I realized that the team had both girls and guys on it. I didn't know they competed equally, and I wanted to make sure the three girls on the team got fair coverage. Maybe talking to Mike about the rifle team could help me break the ice about what I really needed to talk to him about.

I snuck another peek. He was hunched over his keyboard, typing away. Maybe I shouldn't bother him. I started to open up another file on my computer but stopped myself. I needed to find some backbone. I sat up tall in my chair and grabbed a notepad and a pencil. I didn't need the props, but I grabbed them anyway for security.

The wheels of my chair squeaked, announcing my journey to Mike's station. "Hey, Mike, you got a minute?"

He saved his document and said, "Of course. Anything for you."

I swallowed. He wasn't making this easy. "I, uh, notice that we share a team."

"We do?"

"Rifle."

"Oh, yeah. They're mixed. Okay, what do you want to do?"

I shifted slightly in my chair. "Oh, uh, I don't know. I guess we could share the space."

"Yeah, that sounds good. What about reporters?"

"I had Mary Schneider assigned to the team, but we can use your reporter if you want."

"No, Jason Whitney was doing both boys' basketball and rifle, so I'll just go ahead and pull him off rifle. I don't think he was that interested in it anyway." He winked at me as if including me in some kind of inside joke.

Oh, my God. I had to stop this whole thing before Mike went any further. And not just for my sake, but for his, too.

I swallowed again, hard, not sure how to say what I needed to say. "All right. I'll let Mary know that she's flying solo on the rifle team. And I, uh, wanted to thank you for a nice time on Friday."

He beamed at me, and I could see his cheeks flush.

"But I have to tell you. I, uh…" God, this sucked. I looked into his expectant eyes and cringed. *Just say it,* I screamed at myself. "Mike, I just want to be friends. Okay? I hope you can deal with that. Gail pushes too hard sometimes. I like you, but just as a friend." I knew I was kind of babbling, but I had to get it all out before Mike said anything.

He folded his arms, and I could see him processing what I'd just told him. After a moment, he sat up straighter in his chair and pushed a couple of inches away from me. I felt bad for hurting him, but like Gail said to me on the phone, it was better not to lead him on.

"Okay," he said after a long pause. "I'm down with that. I kind of had a feeling anyway."

I grimaced for his benefit. "I'm sorry. But I meant what I said about staying friends. You're a great guy, and I'm sure there's somebody out there for you. Somebody great. It's just not me."

"Okay." He nodded his head toward his computer. "I should get back to this wrestling article. And besides, I think Mrs. Gibson is patrolling."

Mrs. Gibson hovered over one of the kids on the other side of the room. "Oops, yeah. I'd better get back. Thanks, Mike."

"No problem."

I wheeled back to my computer, annoyed that eleventh grade was getting so hard. All the hurdles. I was tired of jumping.

~~~

Gail and I had the lunch table to ourselves because Joey was making up a physics lab or something.

"Great sports section in the paper today, Editor Raines." Gail tapped the open newspaper in front of her.

"Thanks. Everybody seems to think so." I plopped into the chair next to her. "I've been so nervous all day."

"Yeah, your first editing job is kind of big."

"And I, uh, talked with Mike this morning."

She thrust the paper aside and looked at me with expected eyes. I had her full attention.

"How'd he take it?"

I almost laughed in her face. She just loved drama. "He took it okay, I guess. I don't know. I never broke up with anyone before."

She laughed. "You guys weren't even going out, so how could you break up?" Something seemed to dawn on her, and she asked hurriedly, "You haven't gone out with anyone before, have you?"

"No. You know I haven't."

"Phew."

"Why 'phew' again?"

"Because I don't want to miss that. I just want to see you happy."

131

"I haven't ever gone out with anyone, so why are you asking?"

"Hmm. Let's see." She tapped her index finger on the side of her jaw and said, "You kept this other secret of yours from me for four years. Four years!" Although she said it in a joking tone, I knew she was kind of serious.

"Oh, quit. I haven't kept anything else from you." *Except Rebecca.* "I don't have a secret lifestyle or anything." Not really.

"You know. I thought you liked Chris Spencer. Remember him in sixth grade? You always wanted to hang out with him."

I had to laugh. "Chris Spencer? Oh, my God. I just wanted to ride his bike."

Gail laughed with me. "His bike? I can't believe we hung out with him all those times, and all you wanted to do was ride his—" She laughed and then finished her sentence. "Ride his ride. Oh, man. I could have sworn you liked him."

"Chris? No. Sorry."

"And you know what? I just figured something out." Gail looked rather smug. "You like Jessica Alba, don't you?"

I didn't say a word, but I knew my grin would tell her all she needed to know.

Gail pushed me with her shoulder. "Oh, my God. I should have seen it! All those stupid magazines. I thought you liked the flame guy, and all this time, you were in love with the invisible girl."

And Gail didn't know how right she was. Rebecca was turning into the invisible girl right here at Grasse River High School. Lately, I'd only seen her during French class, and she barely spoke to me even then. But that was going to change when *Operation Black-and-White* began later.

I looked around the cafeteria, hopeful that Grasse River's new invisible girl would actually show up. I couldn't look too long because I didn't want to catch Jessie's eye. Oh, I knew Jessie was in the cafeteria. I developed a kind of self-defense radar about her. That's why I stayed in the crowds in the hallways and went straight to all my classes. I became as fast as a NASCAR pit crew when changing my books at my locker. Constantly looking over my shoulder was getting pretty tiring, though. I wish Rebecca would talk to me so I could tell her about Jessie wanting to beat me up. Maybe she could get her to back off or something.

Gail interrupted my thoughts. "Hey. You like someone, don't you?"

I couldn't lie to her. "Yeah, I guess." I felt myself blush.

"Who is she?" Gail grabbed my arm as she scanned the cafeteria.

"You don't know her." Actually, I didn't know if Gail knew Rebecca or not, but I just wasn't ready to reveal my crush just yet. I mean, I wasn't even sure if I could get anywhere with Rebecca anyway. She'd kind of turned me down last week when I'd asked her out. So…yeah. There was no chance.

"C'mon, try me. Is she here? In the cafeteria?"

Talking like this with Gail felt weird, really weird, but it felt oddly freeing at the same time. "No, she hasn't been here since…"

Gail leaned in closer, always ready for good gossip. "Ooh, drama. She hasn't been here since what?"

"Since she broke up with her girlfriend last week."

"Oh, my God. I can't believe there are, like, lesbians at Grasse River. That's so…"

"What?" I wasn't sure if she was going to say "gross" or "disgusting" or "creepy."

"Cool," Gail finally said. "That's so cool. Who knew? It's like a covert operation or something. Oh, my God. And there must be gay guys around here, too." She looked around the cafeteria with her eyes wide. "Ooh, do you think Frank's gay? He's kind of feminine."

God, I had unleashed a madwoman. "I don't know. It's not like we have secret decoder rings or something."

"Okay, so tell me this. We've eaten lunch in this cafeteria practically every day this year, last year, and the year before that, and during that whole time, you've been checking out some hot chick?"

I blushed furiously. "Keep your voice down. But yeah. Well, yes and no. Just the last couple of weeks, I guess."

"And how is it that I've never noticed you doing this?"

I tried my best to plaster a look of disbelief on my face as I said, "One word. Joey."

She scrunched up her face. "Yeah, I guess I am preoccupied, but I like him so much it almost hurts."

I sighed and said, "I know the feeling."

"Oh, Dev, you got it bad. C'mon, who is it?"

I looked at her with the most serious expression I could come up with. "Not yet, okay? I'm still kind of new at this whole thing."

She tried her best boo-boo face on me, but I wasn't Joey. Unlike Joey, I was fairly immune to the Gail Marsters boo-boo face. "Nice try."

She shrugged. "Oh, well. It still works on Joey."

"Speaking of Joey." I pointed as he made his way toward us. Gail's face lit up when she spotted him. I felt a momentary twinge of envy. Would I ever have someone in my life that would make my face light up like that? Or, better yet, would someone ever look at me that way?

~~~

I practically held my breath, waiting for Rebecca to come into the French class. I was torn about implementing *Operation Black-and-White*. I mean, on the one hand, she had told me that she wouldn't go out with me, but on the other hand, my crush on her was reaching monumental proportions, and I had to know for sure once and for all.

A new black and white panda bear sat squarely in the middle of her chair.

My heart raced when Rebecca finally came through the door. I kept my head down as if mesmerized by my French notes but used my peripheral vision to watch her. She stopped short, and I knew she must have been looking at the bear. I tilted my head slightly so I could see her better.

"How cute." She picked up the bear and hugged him.

Aha, the scoreboard clicked over in my favor again, but I hoped the points counted this time.

"Is this from you?" She asked and hugged the bear again.

I nodded. I was sure my voice would betray me if I tried to speak, so I didn't try.

She smiled even bigger as she placed her backpack on the floor between us. "She's adorable. *Merci.*"

I cleared my throat and said, "You're welcome." My stomach flipped over once, but in a good way.

Mme Depardieu tapped on the whiteboard with her marker. "*Écoutez, s'il vous plaît.*" She turned on the radio, and an old pop song from the eighties was playing. She adjusted the volume and then stepped back.

I looked at Rebecca with questions in my eyes and mouthed, "What is she doing?"

Rebecca shrugged her shoulders and looked back down at her notebook.

Mme Depardieu stood at the whiteboard with the black marker in her hand while the radio played on her desk. A commercial came on when the song finished, and then I understood. Mme Depardieu had the radio tuned to a French station from Québec. The song had been in English, but all the commercials were in French. And when the DJ got back on the air, she spoke French as well.

Mme Depardieu looked at all of us expectantly. I guess she figured we'd be as excited about the French radio station as she was.

When another song came on, this one in French, Mme Depardieu turned off the radio. "French radio. I want you all to leesen to it. Leesen to the language flowing over zee airwaves. *Ecoutez* to zee language spoken outside of zis classroom. *Ecoutez* and absorb zeh sound."

She wrote on the board, "Homework Assignment: 1. Find a French radio station." She started to write down the station numbers but shook her head. She said out loud, "No, you can find one on your own. Zare are several." She continued to write on the board. "2: Listen for at least ten minutes. 3. Write down at least two topics from the commercials or DJ. In French."

Mme Depardieu said, "Make sure zat you hear some French during your ten minutes. I wanted to make it twenty, but I'm afraid your parents might not want you to listen to zeh radio for so long."

I had to laugh. Mme Depardieu shortened our homework assignment because she was afraid our parents would object. I think she gave our parents way too much power. Oh, well, I'd take it. I had a lot of other homework on top of the boys' basketball game, which I had to go to later. I was going to interview Tiffany Bridges, the captain of the cheerleading squad. Funny how I assigned myself this particular interview.

I stole a glance at Rebecca. She didn't look my way, though. My heart filled with hope when I saw her clutching the panda bear with her left hand while she wrote down the assignment with her right.

When the bell rang to end the class, Rebecca tucked the panda carefully on top of the books in her backpack. She smiled at me and said, "The sports section in the paper was awesome this morning."

"Thanks," I said and smiled.

"And thanks for the bear. I'll see you later. I have to go to rehearsal." She smiled again.

I watched her leave the classroom, and my stomach got all googly. God, she was so beautiful. I loved everything about her. Even her hands—they were so slim and gentle. I wished I could hold them again. Her skin looked so smooth that I hoped someday I could reach out and touch her cheek. Her lips looked soft enough to kiss. And her eyes—.

I stopped my thoughts with a sudden realization. I clamped my lips shut and put my head down on the desk as things became crystal clear. Who was I to think that someone as beautiful as Rebecca Washington would ever be interested in a plain Jane like me? Even if I were Black, she still wouldn't like me. I mean, she had gone out with Jessie Crowler. I couldn't compete with that. She had taken the panda just to be nice. She must think I'm so pathetic. Oh, my God. I had just embarrassed myself so badly but hadn't even realized it until now.

My eyes welled up with tears, and I took a deep breath to keep them at bay. I was an idiot to think that *Operation Black-and-White* would do any good at all. As reality set in, I think my heart broke all over again.

Chapter 14

Skunk Day

I stood in front of my grandparents' double headstone and pulled my coat tighter around me. I let my mom have her time with Grandma and Grandpa first and now she sat in the car while I had my turn. My mom got a call earlier in the day that the headstone had been installed, so she picked me up after school so we could see it. When Mme Depardieu took the note from the office aide and walked it back to my seat, my heart started to race because the note told me to meet my mother at the main entrance right after school. But it didn't say why. I thought maybe something had happened to my dad or Missy. Dad didn't work directly with the machinery at Alum Castings because he was middle management, whatever that meant, but still, I didn't know if maybe something had happened to him. I guess I was a little edgy since Grandma's death.

Although it was still afternoon, I had to hurry to get my visit in with my grandparents before it became too dark to see. I squatted down and said, "Hey, Grandma and Grandpa, they put in a nice headstone. You guys would like it." My grandparents' names were etched on the stone ornately, and I traced the outline of my grandmother's name, Mildred B. Raines, absentmindedly. "You guys, I have some news. I came out to Gail. I know, I know, Missy told me not to, but Gail's my best friend. Do you remember her? The one who never stops talking? Well, I actually got her to shut up for once when I told her about me. She was cool about it, too. Go figure. I told her at the mall. But before I told her, I found the neatest snow globe for you, Grandma. I kind of started crying in the middle of the mall." I stopped to force down the emotion creeping up my chest. "I know, right? What a baby. But Gail consoled me, and then I felt better. Mom said that you were probably with me at the mall, and that's why the snow globe caught my eye in the first place. Mom thinks that you and Grandpa are around us all the time and that you guys probably rode in the car with us when we came to the cemetery today. That sounds nice. I kind of hope that's true, but don't go, like, appearing as ghosts or anything. That would freak me out, okay?"

I stood up and brushed the light dusting of snow off the top of the new headstone. "Anyway, you guys, do you remember Rebecca? She brought me here in the hearse a couple of weeks ago. Well, on Monday, I gave her a panda bear, and even though I got really depressed and thought maybe she didn't like me, I decided to keep on giving her one stuffed animal every day. I mean, Grandpa. You always said, 'In for a penny, in for a pound,' right? I think I finally understand what that means, so I just kept going with the stuffies." I traced my Grandpa's name so he wouldn't feel left out. "So anyway, on Tuesday, I gave her a penguin, Wednesday a zebra, Thursday the cow, and last Friday was a whale. That's a lot, isn't it? She seems to like them, but I'm still not sure how she feels about me, and I probably should just leave her alone, but I'd already made up my stubborn mind to give her all of them, so today—today's Monday in case you lost track—I gave her the dalmatian. I have one toy left, and it's a skunk, which I'm going to give her tomorrow. Do you think she'll be insulted by a skunk? Do you think she'll get a restraining order and get me arrested for harassment?" I laughed out loud but then squelched it. Laughing in a cemetery didn't seem respectful.

"Grandma? Rebecca's wrapped all the way around my heart, but she doesn't seem to want me. What do I do?"

I tried to talk to Missy over the weekend, but she didn't have much time for me because her final exams were coming up. I think it was the first time Missy couldn't help me with a problem. And I definitely wasn't ready to confess to Gail about my brief foray into stalking Rebecca with stuffed animals. I'd tell Gail eventually, but if *Operation Black-and-White* didn't work, maybe I'd never confess that stupidity.

"But Grandma," I said out loud, "Rebecca held my hand. Right over there." I looked at the spot where my mom sat in the car. "Rebecca's so far away now, though. Oh, I found out where she goes during lunch. I just came out and asked her in French last week. She has that dance concert—it's this

Friday—and she goes down to the dance studio to rehearse or practice or whatever you call it. She told me she goes to the studio because she doesn't want to see Jessie, but maybe she doesn't want to see me, either. I mean, she *has* to see me in French, but..."

I sighed and knew I'd have to wrap it up soon because the tip of my nose was starting to freeze in the mid-December cold.

"You guys, I think it was more than her kindness toward me that made me fall in love with her. Yeah, I think I'm in love." I smiled. "It's her smile, her laugh, her soft brown eyes. The way she walks. And the way she looks at me sometimes. All those things got into my head and trickled down to my heart. I might have been able to make her go away if she was just in my head, but she isn't. And if my skunk doesn't work tomorrow, then I don't know how I'm going to get her out of my heart."

My head snapped up when I heard a car. Rebecca? No, just a minivan. My heart sank again.

"I have to go, you guys. I love you both. Oh, and if you have any influence up there, can you get Rebecca to like me?"

I turned on my heels and hoped Mom had the heater on high.

~~~

I couldn't believe that my AP U.S. History Teacher, Mrs. Cameron, kept us after the bell. All because some stupid kids were talking. She told us that she was taking back the time we wasted. Teachers sure got cranky about that kind of thing. Unfortunately, Mrs. Cameron had no way of knowing it was skunk day, and now I'd be late for French and wouldn't have a chance to sneak him onto Rebecca's chair. Maybe I'd sneak him into her backpack when she wasn't looking. Either way, I was ready to bolt whenever Mrs. Cameron said the word.

"Please remember," Mrs. Cameron said, her eyes narrowed, "we have a lot of ground to cover, and we cannot waste a moment." She kept us hanging for a few more seconds and then said, "Go!" and pointed toward the door.

You would have thought we were in some kind of track sprint; that's how fast everybody got up and raced toward the door. Unfortunately, everybody trying to get out at the same time created a bottleneck and almost sent me into a frenzy.

Once I got through the door, I ran down the hallway to Mme Depardieu's class. I got in the room just as the late bell rang. Rebecca was already in her seat in the back of the room. Darn.

Rebecca watched me as I made my way to my seat. I almost looked behind me to see if she was looking at someone else because the expression on her face was one that I didn't recognize. She was actually smiling. Even her eyes were smiling. She looked more relaxed than she had in weeks. I couldn't help the smile that grew on my face. It wasn't quite the perma-grin of days gone by, but it was close.

I put my backpack on the floor and was about to climb into my seat when I noticed a white bag on my chair. I picked it up carefully and then sat down quickly because Mme Depardieu was starting to teach.

I leaned toward Rebecca and whispered, "Is this from you?"

She nodded but then looked back up at Mme Depardieu, who had turned on the overhead for the day's lesson. We were going to conjugate more subjunctives. How much fun was that? I couldn't have cared less about verbs. All I wanted to do was rip open that white bag and see what was inside. I held the bag in my hands and tried to gauge the size of it. A box of some kind, a little smaller than my Rubik's cube.

Mme Depardieu rambled on and on and on about, I'm not even sure what. I know I took notes; I always took notes, but this time, I had no idea what I was writing down. My brain wasn't engaged in French. My brain was focused on only two things—the package in my left hand and the way Rebecca had smiled at me when I walked into the room. I kept looking at her whenever Mme Depardieu turned her back to the class, and Rebecca grinned at me every single time. It was like we shared some kind of secret, but I had no idea what that secret was, and I didn't even care. My heart was beating so hard I knew everybody could hear it.

I thought about the skunk in my backpack. Maybe I wouldn't have to use the little stinker after all. And after what seemed like six hundred years, Mme Depardieu finished up the notes from the overhead. She went behind her desk and picked up a plastic milk crate.

I looked at Rebecca and shrugged as if to ask, "What is she up to now?"

Rebecca raised her eyebrows and shook her head as if to say, "I have no idea."

I tried to sneak a peek into the package in my hand, but the paper made too much noise, so I stopped and rested the bag in my lap again.

Mme Depardieu pulled out a stack of homemade CDs and said, "Each one of zees is different. Let me explain what we're going to do once everyone has a handout."

I put my pen down and reached for the handout from the girl in front of me. I had to put my pen down because I still clutched the white bag with my other hand.

Mme Depardieu held up one of the CDs. "On each CD eez a pop song. In French. Last week, you listened to some French radio to get zeh feel for the language outside zee classroom, but zis week, you are going to translate zee lyrics into English. The title of zis song is…" She turned the CD toward her so she could read the title. "…'*Sans Cœur*,' which means Heartless. Hmm, *Je me demande de quoi celle-ci parle.*"

"Anyway," Mme Depardieu continued, "There are different songs to translate. I'll give you zeh sheet with zee French lyrics for your song, and I want you to translate zem into English. We'll start work on zees today." She smiled at us, obviously pleased with her clever assignment. Mme Depardieu always tried to find ways to make learning French interesting. The other kids might not think so, but I thought this was a cool assignment. It beats conjugating the subjunctive on a worksheet any day.

Mme Depardieu said, "*C'est un travail à faire à deux.*"

"Partners?" Rebecca asked with an expectant lilt to her voice.

"Sure." Happy dance.

She moved over until our desks were touching. Mme Depardieu handed out a CD and lyrics sheet to each group and told us to begin the translations. The song Rebecca and I got was named "*Ne me Laisse pas Tomber.*"

"Don't give up on me," Rebecca said.

For a split second, I didn't realize she had simply translated the song title. I thought she was telling me not to give up on her. I mentally rolled my stupid eyes at my stupid self.

Rebecca looked down at the bag in my hand. "Are you ever going to open that?"

I couldn't believe I had forgotten. With Rebecca so close to me, nothing else mattered. I kept the bag under my desk so Mme Depardieu wouldn't see and pulled the box out. The other students in the class were making enough noise so that the crinkling of the bag wasn't that noticeable. My hands shook as I opened the top flap of the box. I held my breath and pulled out a glistening snow globe.

"How did you—"

"I wanted to get you something to remind you of your grandmother."

"But how did you know she liked snow globes?"

"You told me."

"I did?"

She nodded. "That time I took you to see her at Greystone, you were upset because you hadn't brought anything."

"And I mentioned snow globes. Yeah, I remember that. Barely." *Barely because all I could think of was being alone with you.*

I shook the glass ball and watched as the snow settled over a snow-covered cottage surrounded by tiny birds and deer. I don't know how I did it, but I managed not to get choked up.

"Thank you," I said and smiled at her.

She beamed. "I should be the one thanking you. I've been kind of not here lately, and I haven't been a very good friend either. And then you brought me all those stuffed animals, and I think you helped me figure out some stuff."

"Figure out what?"

She pressed her lips together and looked as if she wanted to tell me something, something important, but she just shook her head and looked away. I didn't ask again because I think she had started to cry.

I gently placed the snow globe back in its box and into the white bag. I reached into my backpack and pulled out the skunk. Rebecca was still lost in thought and didn't see me move the stinky little thing under my desk toward her. I placed the skunk in her hand, which startled her back to the present.

"Oh, another one? How many of these do you have?"

"That's the last, I swear, but I was late today."

"Oh, Devon. *Merci. Il est très mignon.* You're very sweet."

She reached over for a hug, and I almost melted into my plastic chair. I knew I must be blushing furiously. Skunk day was turning out to be an excellent day, not sucky at all.

Rebecca sighed and cuddled the skunk. "I've been so out of it. And I've got the dance concert this weekend, too. I hope you're still coming. I hope you don't hate me."

"Why would I hate you?" No chance in heck that I'd ever hate Rebecca. Oh, no.

Rebecca just shrugged, and I sent her my most reassuring smile. "I've been counting the days to your dance concert." Oh, God. I actually just said that out loud, didn't I? What a dork.

"You're coming on Friday?"

"Both Friday and Saturday, probably." I only had to get through two more long days, and then it would finally be the Friday I'd been waiting for since forever.

Whatever had made her teary-eyed before seemed to be gone from her mind because she was smiling again. It was the same smile she'd given me when I walked into the classroom earlier.

The bell rang to end the period, and Rebecca got up quickly. She said she didn't want to be rude, but she had to hurry to get to her dance rehearsal. They were having dress rehearsals in the auditorium the whole week.

"See you tomorrow," I said and shook the bag with the snow globe in it. Something had clearly turned around in Rebecca's mind to make her notice me again.

~~~

The auditorium was packed for the Friday night dance concert. Most of the students sat in the back because regular people from town took the seats in front. I had even seen a St. Lawrence County senior citizen bus in the parking lot as my mom dropped Gail and me off.

I tried to hide my excitement as we searched for seats. Gail saw some friends from school and wanted to sit with them way in the back. Normally, I wouldn't have cared, but this time, I did care. I wanted to be able to see

Rebecca close up, but nothing and no one was going to stop me from reaching that goal. Gail took the hint when I suggested we sit near the front.

We found seats three rows away from the stage and the closed velvety purple curtains. As I sat down, I felt myself trembling. I couldn't imagine what would happen when those mammoth curtains opened and Rebecca emerged.

"Hey," Gail said, opening her program, "if this sucks, can we leave at half-time?"

"I think it's called an intermission, but no, we're not going to leave because it's not going to suck."

"Why are we here again?" She put the program in her lap.

I took a deep breath to steady myself. "Because it's time for me to show you."

"Show me what?" The look on her face told me she was very lost.

"Show you…" I leaned closer and said low, "Who I like."

Her eyes shot open wide. "Oh, yeah?" She sounded as if I'd just told her she'd won a car.

I laughed. "Now, don't go crazy about this, okay? Please?"

"Okay, okay." She nodded vigorously. "This is so exciting."

"I know." We giggled like two little kids.

She picked up her program and turned to the page with the dancers' names. "Which one is she?"

God, I hoped no one overheard our conversation. I pointed to Rebecca's name at the way bottom of her program.

"Right there."

"Rebecca Washington. Never heard of her." Gail said way too loudly.

"Shhh, not so loud," I whispered.

"What?" Gail looked around. "I just said a name. No biggie."

I glared at her with wide eyes as if to tell her that it was a "biggie."

"Okay, okay." She put her hands up in defense. "I'm cool. But I don't know her, do I?"

I shrugged. "I don't know. Maybe not."

A hush fell over the audience as Ms. Adams, Rebecca's dance teacher, stepped onto the stage. She looked so sophisticated with a swirling black skirt and a kind of low-cut red top. She even had her dark hair piled up on her head.

It wasn't a beehive or anything weird like that; it was just elegant. I never realized how pretty Ms. Adams was. Everybody started clapping, and Gail and I did, too.

Ms. Adams tapped the cordless microphone in her hand twice. She said, "Thank you all for coming tonight. The dance troupe has been working hard this semester to bring you their interpretation of *A Night without Bound*. Refreshments will be served at intermission, and you are welcome to enjoy them in the lobby at that time." She looked up to the lighting booth and nodded. "Okay, it seems like we're ready. Again, thank you all for coming, and please enjoy *A Night without Bound*."

The audience clapped again, and I held my breath as the curtains opened. The first number included the entire ensemble. That's what Rebecca had called the whole group—an ensemble.

My heart almost stopped when I saw her glide across the stage to the music. She wore a salmon-colored outfit, kind of revealing, but she looked like a professional dancer. I felt my cheeks get warm as I watched her lithe body move around the stage. She simply glided; there was no other way to describe it.

"Which one is she?" a voice asked in my ear.

I almost swatted Gail away like an annoying gnat, but I caught myself in time. I didn't want to tear my eyes away from Rebecca, but I was the one who had invited Gail to the dance concert, so I had to answer her question.

A group of dancers that didn't include Rebecca were in the middle of the stage doing some kind of ballet spins, pirouettes, I think they were called, while the rest of the dancers stayed off to the sides of the stage and swayed to the music. I tried to be subtle as I pointed to Rebecca on the far side of the stage.

"Who?" Gail yelled in my ear.

I turned and said, "Wait 'til she comes to this side."

"Okay." She fell back against her chair.

The lead dancers finished their pirouettes and melded back in with the rest. The dancers weaved their way in and around each other, and Rebecca ended up near our side of the stage. I pointed to her again; she was right in front of us.

"Which one? The one with the white ribbon?"

Rebecca wore some kind of dark cord around her hair, not a white ribbon. "No, over there."

"Where?"

"Right there." I pointed at Rebecca. I even looked up my own arm and through my finger to make sure I pointed directly at her. When Rebecca moved, my finger followed, but still, Gail didn't seem to see her.

Gail said, "The short girl with the teeth?"

I dropped my arm in frustration. It was as if Gail couldn't see Rebecca at all. Was Rebecca invisible? Then it dawned on me. Gail couldn't see Rebecca because she was Black. Gail was probably looking for a white girl and got confused when I kept pointing to Rebecca.

Gail looked at me and yelled in my ear, "The Black girl?" She said the words with such disbelief that it was like I had pointed to a potted plant.

"Shhh," I hissed at her. The senior citizens in front of us turned around and asked us to keep it down. I apologized, but Gail just sat with her mouth hanging open.

I originally thought Gail would have a hard time accepting the fact that I was gay, but she seemed to be having a harder time accepting the fact that I liked a Black girl. It was as if liking Rebecca wasn't even a possibility in Gail's mind.

I looked at her and nodded. "That's Rebecca. Rebecca Washington."

"You're kidding," she said with disbelief. She acted as if I was joking.

Gail sat back in her seat and didn't say another thing to me during the rest of the first act. Once again, I had managed to make Gail Marsters speechless. Maybe all my recent news had been too much to handle. Maybe now that I had put an actual girl's face to my orientation, she freaked because it had become very real. I decided that Gail would have to work this one out for herself.

Chapter 15

The Invisible Wall

I didn't ask Gail to go with me to Rebecca's concert on Saturday night, so I sat by myself in the third row. Gail didn't text me all day, and I decided not to text her. I wasn't trying to be mean or anything; I just wanted to give her the space she probably needed to figure things out. I almost asked Missy to go with me since she was home for Christmas but decided against it since I wanted to watch Rebecca without distraction. My mom didn't understand why I wanted to go to the dance concert two nights in a row, so I lied and told her that I was covering the dance concerts for the newspaper. Of course, I'd probably get caught in the lie when the article came out with someone else's byline, but I'd cross that bridge when it came to me.

After Dad dropped me off at the auditorium, I bought a dozen red roses in the lobby. I held them in my lap, ready to give to Rebecca after the show. I should have brought her flowers the night before, but, actually, I was kind of glad that I hadn't known about the flowers thing because giving Rebecca flowers might have put Gail right over the edge.

As the last dance number came to a close, the audience burst into thunderous applause. My pulse raced as the velvet curtains closed in front of the dancers. Several people started a standing ovation, so I jumped up, put the roses carefully on my seat, and clapped as loudly as I could. I wished I knew how to do that loud whistle thing where you put two fingers in your mouth. Maybe I could learn before Rebecca's next concert.

Finally, after a hundred years, the curtain opened again, and the dancers pranced their way out one by one. When Rebecca came out, I clapped louder and even yelled, "Whoo hoo." I didn't even care who heard me.

Rebecca didn't make eye contact with me, though, but I could tell the

147

standing ovation and the enthusiastic applause pleased her. The dancers grabbed each other's hands and took a giant group bow. I didn't think it was possible, but the audience clapped even louder. The girls bowed again, acknowledged the people in the lighting booth, and then one of the girls, a senior, I think, ran down the steps and dragged Ms. Adams back on stage. Again, the audience picked up volume. A giant bouquet of flowers emerged from somewhere, and one of the dancer's parents presented it to the dance teacher. Ms. Adams beamed and then bowed to the audience. She turned to face her dancers and bowed to them. That must have been the signal for the dancers to break ranks and swarm their teacher. My hands were getting tired from clapping for so long, but I didn't care because I clapped for Rebecca.

I hung back for a few minutes in my seat after the house lights came on and waited for the right moment to approach Rebecca with my roses. Her family, like most of the other dancers, surrounded her when she stepped down off the stage. Her brother and her parents gave her flowers. I had, unfortunately, seen Jessie during the intermission, but luckily didn't see her now. She must have ducked out when the concert ended.

Rebecca hugged her parents, and as they turned to go, my heart increased speed. I made my way toward her slowly. She had turned to head back up the stairs to the stage, but I stopped her with a tap on her shoulder from behind.

"You were amazing," I said, clutching the flowers tightly.

She turned and smiled. "I saw you in the third row."

"You did?"

"I did," she said softly. "The stage lights light up the first few rows."

I was instantly mortified. Oh my God, I hadn't realized the dancers could see into the audience. Rebecca must have known that I couldn't take my eyes off her. I thrust the flowers toward her to cover my embarrassment.

"For me?" She leaned in for a hug as she took them. She put her hand on my shoulder and whispered, "Thanks for coming. Both nights."

She pulled away, but I still felt the heat of her touch. My heart was pounding when I stammered, "You're welcome. It was—" I couldn't find the right word. "You were awesome," I said instead.

"Thanks, Devon." She juggled both sets of flowers so she could hold them with one arm.

I smiled like an idiot and took pride in the fact that my bouquet was bigger than her parents'.

"Devon?"

"Yeah?" She had me spellbound, standing so close to me in her low-cut dance outfit, perspiration glistening on her skin. I wanted to wrap my arms around her, but then what? I wasn't sure. Probably kiss her. No, definitely. I definitely wanted to kiss her.

"I, uh…," she started, but then seemed at a loss for words. "Can I take you to see your grandma again? Maybe tomorrow?"

"My grandma?" I was confused for a second, but then I realized that Rebecca wanted to take me to the cemetery. The smile that popped out on my face must have given away my answer. My perma-grin was back.

She smiled in response. "Is that a yes, then?"

"Yes. Yes. Yes."

She tapped the tip of my nose with her finger. "Good. Noon, okay?"

"Tomorrow?"

"The sooner the better."

I nodded and tried to remember to breathe. Yeah, sooner was better, even though I might pass out first.

~~~

Right after Saturday's dance concert, I practically dragged Missy to our room to tell her everything because I couldn't keep it in any longer. I even told her about the bad parts with Gail.

She said, "I told you not to tell Gail."

"But—"

"I told you she wouldn't take it well."

"But, Missy," I whined like I was back in elementary school and hugged Grizzly tighter. "She took the gay thing okay."

"She did?"

"Yeah, at the mall. She was cool. She said she wanted to see me happy."

Missy shrugged her shoulders as if she wasn't sure she believed me. "So why was she so cold to you at the dance concert last night?"

149

"Well," and I hated to think this about my best friend, but I said it anyway, "I think Gail has a problem with Rebecca."

"And it can't be because Rebecca's ugly."

My eyes flew wide open, and I grinned. "No, it can't because she ain't!" I laughed with Missy, incredulous that I could talk to my sister about a girl I liked.

"Because Rebecca's a girl?"

"No. I think it's the Black thing."

"Oh." Missy clucked her tongue once in disappointment. "I'm surprised at that. I thought Gail would have trouble with the gay thing, not the Black thing."

"I know. Me, too. But actually…"

"What?"

"I think Rebecca had trouble with the Black thing, too."

Missy took Grizzly from me and held him. "What do you mean?"

"Well, not so much the Black thing, but the white thing." I rubbed my finger on the back of my white hand.

"Uh, oh."

"No, but here's the cool part." I got up and showed Missy the snow globe Rebecca had given me. "Rebecca gave me this on Tuesday."

"Wow." Missy shook the globe. "This is just like the kind Grandma collects. Collected, I mean."

I saw tears well up in my sister's eyes and realized that Missy was still grieving like I was. I sat down next to her on her bed. Maybe this was my chance to help Missy for a change. "But, Missy, here's the cool thing. I think maybe Grandma helped Rebecca and me find each other."

Missy wiped her eyes. "Oh, yeah? And how's that?"

"Okay, uh…" I wasn't sure how Missy would feel about my theory, but I gave it a shot anyway. "Okay, why did we have the wake at Washington Funeral Home? There're like seventy other funeral homes in town."

"More like two," she corrected, but I could tell I had her attention.

"Okay, but why did we have the wake at the Washington's?" I answered my own question. "So I could meet Rebecca."

"Okay, keep going."

"Um, well, you told me about that secluded hallway in the funeral home. Remember that?"

"Yeah."

"That's where I met her. Well, I mean, I kind of knew her from French, but I hadn't met her before. She helped me when I was crying my head off back there."

"Oh, squirt, Rebecca saw you crying?"

"Yeah, and I was going at it, too. It was kind of embarrassing, actually. You know, for a little while, I thought maybe the only reason I had a crush on her was because she helped me at the wake and the funeral."

"Obviously, you changed your mind. How come?"

"She gave me that." I pointed to the snow globe in Missy's hand. "Grandma's been manipulating things from…"

"Heaven? The Great Beyond? The celestial bridge game in the sky?" Missy suggested.

"Yeah." I laughed, and so did Missy.

"Sounds farfetched, squirt, but I have to admit those are a lot of coincidences. And Rebecca's taking you to the cemetery tomorrow?"

"Yeah, and it was her idea."

Missy pursed her lips and nodded. "Her idea, huh? Well, let me know what happens. I'll keep my fingers crossed for you. And, uh, maybe Grandma can help me with my love life, too."

"Why? What happened to Mr. Chemistry major?"

"Oh, well. Let's just say he was more interested in a hit and run."

"A what?" It dawned on me what she meant, and I blushed. "Oh."

The conversation turned at that point, but I was pleased that Missy hadn't made fun of my idea about Grandma helping me find Rebecca.

~~~

When I heard a car pull into the driveway, I stood up from the living room couch so fast I dropped my cell phone on the floor. Missy looked out the front window and nodded at me in affirmation. Her grin was so loud that I widened my eyes to tell her to shut up.

"Mom," I yelled toward the kitchen. "She's here." I pulled my coat on and plunked my ski cap on my head.

"Okay, honey," she said, drying her hands on a dish towel. "I'd tell you to have a good time, but I don't think that's appropriate in this case, is it?"

"I think it's okay because one time I talked to Grandpa about fishing when I was there."

My dad put the Sunday paper down and looked at me. "Fishing?"

"Yeah, Rebecca likes to go fishing, so I told Grandpa about it."

My dad asked, "Worms or lures?" My dad was a lures kind of guy, and it was something he and Grandpa had argued about all the time.

"Um, sorry, Dad. Worms."

He just shook his head and said, "These kids today. Go figure. Fine. Carry on." He picked his paper back up.

"Well," my mom said as she opened the front door for me, "have a good time, then. Tell Grandma and Grandpa we said hello."

I smiled. "Okay."

"Oh, honey," my mom said sharply. "You're going in the hearse?"

Missy started laughing out loud.

I looked out the front storm door. "Apparently." I shrugged with a smile.

"In the snow? Can Rebecca drive that thing in the snow?"

"Of course she can, Mom," I said in my best reassuring voice, even though I had no idea if Rebecca could drive a hearse in the snow. All I knew was that I had to get out of the house quickly.

My mom frowned for a moment as if wondering if I had lost my mind, but then she just shook her head and said, "Go on, but make sure you come right back. Don't go driving around town in that thing." She gave me a quick hug.

"Don't worry, Mom. We won't."

"Good luck, squirt," Missy teased.

I shot Missy another wide-eyed look and then completely ignored her as I said, "Bye, Mom. Bye, Dad." I trotted out the door and let my mom close it behind me. I hadn't realized that the snow was sticking. The world looked covered by a soft white blanket, all peaceful and calm. I wasn't calm, though, when I opened the door to the hearse idling in the driveway.

"Hi," I said to Rebecca as I got in.

"Hi, yourself," Rebecca answered. "Ready to go?"

"Yup. No caskets?"

"No caskets."

Rebecca backed out and headed toward the cemetery.

She was oddly quiet, so I tried to fill the space. "You guys were amazing this weekend."

"Thanks. Was that your first dance concert?"

I nodded. "I'm ashamed to say that, yeah, it was my first time."

"Well, thanks for coming. I, for one, appreciate the support. Did you see Jessie on Saturday?"

Hearing Jessie's name made me feel like I'd been punched in the stomach. Why did she have to go and bring her up? "Yeah," was all I could say.

"I saw her in the audience, too. But I'm glad she didn't try to give me flowers or anything."

"Me, too," I said and was shocked at my boldness.

Rebecca looked at me and said softly, "But I'm glad *you* did."

"Give you flowers?"

"Yeah. My parents were relieved when I told them they weren't from Jessie. They don't like her, either."

I laughed. I guess my disdain for the basketball wonder was no secret from her. I just wondered if Rebecca knew how much Jessie tortured me. "Did you tell your parents who they were from?"

"Nope. Not yet."

"Do they know about you?"

"That I like girls?"

I nodded.

"Yes, they know."

She didn't elaborate as we pulled into the Greystone cemetery. She maneuvered the immense hearse down the tree-lined road that brought us to my grandparents' gravesites. I never realized how tranquil the cemetery looked, covered in snow.

She pulled the hearse up to the same spot as last time and put it in park. She said, "I'll keep the engine running for the heater, but please don't think I'm rushing you."

"Okay." I got out of the hearse to pay my respects and walked up to my grandparents' side-by-side graves. I brushed the wet snow off the top of the pretty rose-colored headstone and took a deep breath.

"Grandma, did you see the snow globe Rebecca got me? It's a sign, isn't it? I know you had something to do with it. Oh, my God, I'm so freakin' nervous. Oh, sorry. *Freakin'* really isn't a curse, though."

I looked toward Rebecca where she sat in the hearse. Like the last time, she didn't look my way. Thank God. That would have made me even more nervous than I already was. Even my hands were sweating inside my gloves.

"You guys," I said to the headstone, "can you maybe not watch when I get back in the hearse with Rebecca? I mean, we might say some personal stuff. Maybe you guys could play bridge. You can play bridge in heaven, right?"

I sighed and said, "Well, I love you guys. Mom and Dad say hi. Missy, too." I wrapped my arms around myself and let the memories of my grandparents overtake me. I teared up a little because I was missing them, but I also had this warm, glow-like feeling in my chest at the same time. My mom said that we still had Grandma and Grandpa in our memories. She was right. I took in the headstone for a few more seconds and then said, "Okay, I'm going back to the hearse now. And you guys are going to play bridge, right? Right."

The wet snow clung to my boots as I walked back toward the black hearse. It looked like Mother Nature had spread white icing on top of it. My adrenaline must have been working overtime because I wasn't even cold. Rebecca had the heat turned up so high that her jacket was undone, and her gloves were off. I took mine off, too.

Rebecca turned toward me. "Finished already?"

"Yeah. They weren't very talkative today."

She laughed and then smiled at me in such a way that I swear my boots melted. She made no move to put the hearse in drive. In fact, she even took off her seatbelt. I took that as a cue to keep mine off as well. The snow that covered the windshield made me feel safe and snug inside our own private cocoon.

An awkward silence overtook us, but then Rebecca smiled as if she suddenly remembered something. "Oh, oh, oh! I got the letter."

"What letter?"

"They want my audition DVD."

"Who does?"

"The Karen Swanson School of Dance in New York. The summer program."

"Ahhh," I squealed with her and reached my arms out for a congratulatory hug. She hugged me back, and when the squealing was done, I started to pull away, but Rebecca didn't. She kept her arms wrapped tightly around me. Inch-by-inch, the smile on her face turned serious, and I almost forgot to breathe.

She leaned her face toward mine. I looked into her eyes. My heart pounded as she inched forward and touched her lips to mine. Her lips were as soft as I imagined. She kissed me gently at first, tentatively, but I kissed her back with a passion I was just beginning to discover. Something deep inside of me woke up, and I pulled her even closer, trying to get all of her at once.

We dragged ourselves away from each other breathless.

"I hope that was okay," she said, her voice breaking.

I laughed. "Do you hear me complaining?" I reached up and stroked her cheek like I had imagined doing in French class. "So soft."

She blushed and kissed the palm of my hand. I couldn't believe how amazing it felt to have the palm of your hand kissed.

"Devon," Rebecca said in between kisses, "I want to say so much to you." She grabbed the hand she'd been kissing and held it. "First, though, I have a small confession."

"Hmm?"

"When my mom asked me to assist at a wake one Wednesday evening, I looked at the name, and my heart broke." Rebecca rubbed the back of my hand. "I wasn't sure if it was someone in your family, but I wanted to be there to help you if I could."

"Help me?"

"My heart broke again when I saw you walk in. You looked so dazed and just, I don't know, devastated."

"I was," I said to her. "I still am."

"I know. I know." She rubbed my hand again. "I kind of followed you covertly when you went into the back hallway."

"You were stalking me?" I asked with a chuckle.

"Mm hmm." Rebecca's embarrassed grin was heart-melting. "Devon, I've liked you since school started this year."

"You have?"

Rebecca nodded and looked down, obviously embarrassed. "I didn't know how to tell you, and I couldn't anyway since I was with someone."

"Wow, wow, wow," I said. I was having a hard time processing this new bit of information.

"You walk with such confidence, and you're always prepared for class. It's like you really take school seriously. And I love that."

"I'm not so sure about the confidence thing."

Rebecca chuckled. It was a low, evil kind of chuckle. "Believe me. It's there."

I swallowed hard, not sure what to say next, but then she continued. "Devon, listen, the Black/white thing does not matter. We're all just souls in a meat locker. It took a while to figure out, but I like Devon Raines's soul, no matter what color her meat locker is."

Yay, my inner voice rejoiced inside me.

"I let my friends and Jessie influence me too much," Rebecca continued. "It's funny," she said with a sigh, "when I dance, I put myself out there, but in other aspects, I'm scared to death."

Rebecca seemed to get choked up, so I didn't say anything for a while. After almost twenty seconds of silence, I finally asked her, "What are you scared of?"

"I'm worried about what people think about me, for one. And I've never been able to stand up to Jessie. Not really." She looked up at me as if searching for strength.

I put on the bravest face I had and hoped she'd never know that I had no idea how to stand up to Jessie, either. "Oh, don't worry about her. She's not a problem anymore, is she?"

"No, I guess not. She was always more talk than action, anyway." She kissed my palm again. "But I was so pig-headed, and I'm truly sorry for that. That was *not* me, and I'm not letting you get away from me again." She looked down at our hands and then squeezed mine. "If that's okay with you."

I simply nodded, speechless. Of course, I didn't want her to let me go. I'd probably hang on even if she tried to.

"Devon, I'm so grateful you kept persisting. You were relentless, you know."

"I was?"

"Yeah, you'd look at me during French with those baby brown eyes of yours and those pink cheeks and that smile. And then you started giving me all those black and white stuffed animals. I did get it, you know, Black and white. Very clever. I didn't want to ignore you during French, but I thought it would be better for both of us if I did."

"Why? You were so confusing. Sending mixed messages."

"I know. I'm sorry. Well, like I said, my friends gave me a lot of grief about hanging out with the *white girl*. And…"

"And, what?"

"And I think I stayed away because I didn't want Jessie harassing you."

Too late, I thought, but said instead, "I can take care of myself." Hopefully, Jessie really was all talk and no action.

"I know you can. I'm glad. But it was so hard to stay away from you when all I wanted to do was hold you and kiss you and think about being with you."

"You did?" I swallowed hard. My heart sang all on its own.

"I mean, I wasn't sure if my attraction to you had deepened out of sympathy for your grandma, but when I couldn't get you out of my mind, I knew."

"It was the same for me. I wasn't sure at first either."

She nodded. "And you know what else?"

"What?"

"I hate beer."

"Oh, my God, me, too. So why did you drink so much that night at Bruster?"

"'Cuz you were right there so close in the car with us, and I kind of panicked, I guess. And maybe I thought I could let you know how I felt if I was drunk enough."

"I knew you were sending me a sign!"

"When I stumbled against you in the woods? Oh, yeah, Ms. Devon Raines, that was intentional. It was a big flashing neon sign, but then I had to get back in the car with Jessie." Rebecca flashed me that sad smile again but continued, "I'm so glad you didn't give up on me. Somehow, you found me on the other side of my invisible wall."

"The Black and white wall."

"Yeah. I don't know why people are such jerks. Why can't people just be people? Not Black, not white, not whatever—just people."

"Just souls in different colored meat suits," I said with a laugh. She smiled at me, and then I said, "But it's not that simple, is it? Being Black or being white is more than skin color, isn't it?"

"Yeah," she said succinctly.

"I mean, it comes with heritage and ancestors and history. Lots of history. And you can't just dismiss ethnicity or race."

Rebecca nodded as she absorbed what I was saying. "You're getting very philosophical, Devon."

"I know," I continued. "I'm sorry. Do you remember that pregnant lady in the mall?"

"Which—"

"Remember? 'Diluting the blood, man.'" I mimicked Jessie. "The Black guy and the white woman?"

"Oh, yeah. What about them?"

"Her baby. Is her baby going to be white or Black? I mean, the baby's going to be mixed."

"Well, sometimes Blacks can pass for white."

"What does that mean, though? Why does a person have to *pass* for white? Do whites *pass* for Black? I agree with you about people just being people thing. But the word *people* means all kinds of different things." My thoughts were swirling around my head so fast that I blew out a sigh and squeaked, "Aaah, this is so confusing."

"I know. Now you see why I had to take some time to get it figured out in my own head."

"You know what?" I asked her.

"What?"

"We're not that different, you and me." I pulled up my jacket sleeve and motioned for her to do the same. I placed my white forearm against her dark one. "We're just different shades, is all." I rubbed my arm on hers. "See, we even feel the same."

She laughed, but then I reached down for her hand, and I kissed her fingertips one at a time. "I think that Blacks and whites and yellows and reds and browns will only be able to overlook their differences when aliens invade Earth."

She laughed. "Aliens?"

"Yeah, then we'll all have to become the human race and not the Black race or the white race or whatever."

"Good theory, but I don't have as much faith in people as you do."

I smiled at her, knowing this was probably the first of many more conversations we'd have on this topic. We were quiet for a moment until she commented on the snow accumulating on the windows and suggested that maybe she should take me home.

"No, no no. Not yet!" I squeezed her hand with both of mine and blurted, "Rebecca, I think about you all the time, and I don't even care if Jessie beats me up. Every morning when I get up, all day long, and before I go to sleep, I think about you. I think about things I want to tell you during French. I think about what it would be like to touch your cheek. I just…I just—" I ran out of words and started to choke up.

"Shhh." She gently touched a finger to my lips. "I know. I already know, Devon."

She slid her finger down my lips, circled my chin, and then put her arms around my neck. I put my own around her waist and pulled her closer until our noses touched. I tilted my head to one side so I could kiss her. With a boldness I didn't know I had, I reached under her coat and touched her warm back. She moaned, and I took that as encouragement, so I caressed her back while we kissed.

We finally broke apart. I melted when I saw the look of love reflected in her gentle brown eyes.

I know my expression turned quite serious when I said, "I've got a tough question for you."

"I'm pretty sure I can handle anything at this point, so go ahead."

"Who are we going to eat lunch with?"

She smiled. "I guess we'll have to start our own table."

I nodded in agreement and said, "That'll be quite an undertaking."

"But we'll do it together, right?"

"Yeah, we will. And what about Jessie?"

"We'll do that together, too."

I believed her as she flashed me her most reassuring smile. I let her kiss me again as the snow buried us against the world.

~~~ The End ~~~

Resources

lgbt national help center
https://lgbthotline.org/

From the lgbt national help center website:

"All of our support volunteers identify as part of the LGBTQIA+ family, and are here to serve the entire community, by providing free & confidential peer-support, information, and local resources through national hotlines and online programs."

LGBT National Hotline: 888-843-4564
LGBT National Coming Out Support Hotline: 888-688-5428
LGBT National Youth Talkline: 800-246-7743
LGBT National Senior Hotline: 888-234-7243

About the Author

Barbara L. Clanton

Barbara L. Clanton is a native New Yorker who left those "New York minutes" for a slower-paced life in central Florida. While in middle and high schools, she played any sport she could find—softball, volleyball, basketball, and field hockey. During high school, she could even be found in the upstairs gym playing handball with her friends. She played softball at Princeton University and was the team captain during her Ivy League champion senior year.

She has spent her career teaching computer science and mathematics at college preparatory schools in New York and Florida. She also coached softball and basketball in both states as well. As an amateur softball player, she was inducted into the ASANA's (Amateur Sports Alliance of North America) Hall of Fame.

Somewhere in adulthood, she picked up a new hobby. "Dr. Barb" plays the bass guitar and has been in several pop-rock bands, playing in notable events such as Gay Days Orlando.

When asked why she started writing, she said she was writing the books she wished she had in high school to help her make sense of her "differentness." Although the world is evolving, it's still not easy to come out to yourself or the world. She hopes her books will help.

Barbara L. Clanton's Instagram:
https://www.instagram.com/barbara.clanton14

Barbara L. Clanton's Goodreads Page:
https://www.goodreads.com/author/show/3072442.Barbara_L_Clanton

Barbara L. Clanton's Author Page on Amazon:
https://www.amazon.com/Barbara-L-Clanton

Books by Barbara L. Clanton

THE GRASSE RIVER SERIES (Young Adult)

The Grasse River Series follows two high school juniors who discover their mutual attraction for each other. The problem? There are a few. They're both girls. They're from different social groups. And one of them is already in a relationship. To compound it, they live in a small town where there seem to be unwritten but clear expectations about who you can be and what you can do. The fact that Grasse River High School even has lesbian students has everyone in a twitter. And once that news is out, Devon gets harassed about having "jungle fever" because she is white and Rebecca is Black. Rebecca gets harassed about being an "Aunt Jemima," accused of latching on to a white girl for the boost it can give her. Although they don't want to, it might be easier to just go back to their respective expected lanes. With that spoken wedge placed firmly between them, neither one is sure their relationship will withstand it.

Quite an Undertaking: Devon's Story
(Book One in the Grasse River Series)
A young adult interracial lesbian romance

Devon Raines, a sixteen-year-old journalism nerd, was happily minding her own business when, wham, her life was turned upside down. She struggled with grief when her grandmother died from a sudden heart attack. But it was at her grandmother's wake that she locked eyes with the most beautiful Black girl she'd ever seen. No, Rebecca Washington was the most beautiful *girl* she'd ever seen, period. Would this beautiful dancer freak out if she knew Devon was gay and attracted?

Enter Jessie Crowler, Rebecca's basketball-playing best friend. Or were they only friends? Devon tried to hide her attraction for the ebony dancer, but would fate allow Rebecca to look her way? Would Jessie get in the way? Would the difference in skin color keep them apart? All this adds up to quite an undertaking in Devon's formerly quiet existence.

ISBN: 978-1-953734-38-9 (eBook)
ISBN: 978-1-953734-39-6 (Paperback)

Rebecca's Story (Book Two in the Grasse River Series)
< Coming Soon >

THE WHICKETT SERIES (Young Adult & New Adult)

The Whickett Series follows two young women who discover a close friendship. For Meredith, their friendship has always been about friendship and nothing more. For Danielle, it has always been about more, but she respects the friendship and resigns herself to remaining friend-zoned because it's a way to keep Meredith in her life. This series starts following the two young women in their second semester of senior year in high school. Book one is the young adult novel: "Art for Art's Sake: Meredith's Story." The series continues into their first semester of college in the new adult novel: "More Than Roommates: Dani's Story." Somewhere along the way, their definition of friendship changes.

Art for Art's Sake: Meredith's Story (Book One in the Whickett Series)
A young adult lesbian romance.

High school senior Meredith Bedford is a social outcast. Her family recently moved from the Catskill Mountains to the sprawling suburbs of Albany, the capital of New York State. Shy and self-conscious about her acne scars, she stays to herself and tries to remain invisible. Her twelve-year-old brother, Mikey, has Down Syndrome, and she tries hard not to blame her troubles on him. Despite verbal and sometimes physical harassment, she survives because she has her art. She was selected to be part of the elite Advanced Placement art class and is quite good at capturing the emotions of her subjects in her portraits. Besides her family, art is the one thing that helps her cope with her outcast status.

One day, at a senior class meeting, she sees Dani Lassiter, president of the senior class and captain of the lacrosse team, and she knows that she must paint this enigmatic young woman. One class period later, Dani manipulates things to have Meredith as her partner for a history project. Meredith is suspicious of Dani's motives but takes a chance. And it pays off. Meredith slowly sheds her invisibility cloak and allows Dani in - a little at a time. They explore an old Victorian house for their history project and become close with Esther and Millie, the two older women who own the house and who've lived together for about forty years. But, when Dani reveals to Meredith that she is gay, Meredith simply can't deal with the news. How had she not known? What is it that won't allow her to come to terms with this unexpected news? Will Meredith control her own homophobia, or will she reject the one person who had taken a chance on her and made her feel human?

ISBN: 978-1-953734-34-1 (eBook)
ISBN: 978-1-953734-35-8 (Paperback)

More Than Roommates: Dani's Story
(Book Two in the Whickett Series)

A new adult lesbian romance.

This new adult lesbian romance is the story of Danielle (Dani) Lassiter as she heads off to Syracuse University for her freshman year of college. And as far as any of their new college friends know, she and her girlfriend Meredith are just roommates and nothing more. And for a little while, they are able to keep it their private secret.

Dani has goals for her college career. She wants to get involved in campus politics and get elected as one of the freshmen representatives of the Student Association. She's also set her sights on improving her lacrosse skills so she can be good enough to make the varsity women's lacrosse team.

Reality hits hard and fast, though, when she discovers that things aren't coming as easily to her in college as they did in high school. An older female student assaults her. A lacrosse coach tells her she isn't good enough. And, the worst thing, her relationship with her not-just-a-roommate Meredith lands on shaky ground from both sides.

Dani accidentally starts an informal after-school program teaching young neighborhood children lacrosse. At one point, she advises them to just "be themselves." She tells them that good things will happen if they do that. It is only when ten-year-old Natalie reminds her to do that for herself that she becomes unsure of what it means to "be herself." Who is Danielle Lassiter, really? Unsteady and unsure, Dani has difficult decisions to make. And one of those decisions includes whether or not she should stay at Syracuse University. Running away to Albany State might be easier on everyone, including herself.

ISBN: 978-1-953734-36-5 (eBook)
ISBN: 978-1-953734-37-2 (Paperback)

THE CLARKSONVILLE SERIES (Young Adult)

The Clarksonville Series follows four high school girls in upstate New York as they maneuver the difficult process of coming out to themselves, each other, and their families. And it doesn't always go well. The four friends have a mutual love of softball, which helps them bond and find love. Each book is from a different character's point of view, but all four main characters are present in each book. There are currently eight books in the series.

Out of Left Field: Marlee's Story
(Book One in the Clarksonville Series)

A young adult lesbian romance.

High school junior Marlee McAllister lives and breathes softball. She's the pitcher for the Clarksonville Cougars in the North Country of upstate New York. With the season opener approaching, Marlee and her best friend, Jeri D'Amico, go to scout their rivals, the East Valley Panthers. The Panthers' star pitcher, Christy Loveland, took the All-county pitching title the preceding year. It is a title Marlee covets. Marlee and Jeri settle in for the game, but as the Panthers take the field, Marlee finds herself staring at Susie Torres, the Panther left fielder.

For reasons Marlee doesn't understand, she's drawn to Susie. Over the next few weeks, Marlee and Susie will slowly act on their mutual attraction. But suddenly, Susie pulls away without explanation, and Marlee realizes it has to do with Christy. Susie won't explain the bond she and Christy share, but whatever it is, it threatens Marlee's burgeoning relationship with Susie.

Struggling to maintain her grades, dealing with the ever-increasing estrangement from her best friend Jeri, and handling the pressures of the All-county pitching competition, Marlee also has to confront the bittersweet realities of what it might mean to be gay.

ISBN: 978-1-953734-04-4 (eBook)
ISBN: 978-1-953734-16-7 (Paperback)

Tools of Ignorance: Lisa's Story
(Book Two in the Clarksonville Series)

A young adult lesbian romance.

Lisa Brown is the starting catcher for the Clarksonville Cougars High School softball team, and she has a major crush on her pitcher, Marlee. Lisa continues to carry her torch for Marlee, even when Sam, a rival softball player, flirts sweetly. However, Lisa becomes more confused than ever when Tara, the first girl she ever kissed and the first girl who ever broke her heart, resurfaces. Since Marlee doesn't know Lisa's alive, should Lisa give up on her once and for all?

Sam seems to have secrets of her own, but Lisa wonders if she should overlook them and allow her fledging attraction to grow for the pretty blonde, or should she fan the tiny flame still burning in her heart for Tara? Lisa faces these problems and deals with society's tools of ignorance in her quest for love and acceptance.

ISBN: 978-1-953734-06-8 (eBook)
ISBN: 978-1-953734-17-4 (Paperback)

Going, Going, Gone: Susie's Story
(Book Three in the Clarksonville Series)

A young adult lesbian romance.

Susie Torres planned to spend most of the summer before her senior year of high school with her girlfriend, Marlee McAllister, but that's proving to be quite challenging. Marlee works at D'Amico's restaurant, and Susie babysits for Mrs. Johnson, her mother's boss. Susie hates the job because she not only works like a slave but almost gets paid like one. Susie is desperate to take her physical relationship with Marlee further, but she knows she has to go at Marlee's slower pace. Complicating things is the attention that a pretty blonde softball player from another team shows Marlee, and Susie falls into a funk when Marlee seems to enjoy it.

On top of that, nothing she does seems to be good enough for her summer softball coach. Frustrated with life, Susie accidentally, on purpose, comes out to her mother. It would be an understatement to say that her mother didn't take it well. Can Susie deal with a girlfriend whose head has possibly been turned by another, an employer who treats her like dirt, a coach who doesn't respect her, and a mother who tells her she is unnatural? Can she get her life back on track before senior year starts?

ISBN: 978-1-953734-05-1 (eBook)
ISBN: 978-1-953734-18-1 (Paperback)

Stealing Second: Sam's Story
(Book Four in the Clarksonville Series)
A young adult lesbian romance

Samantha Rose Payton likes girls, but her parents don't know that. And Sam would like to keep it that way because her parents are ultra-conservative Republicans. They live in a mansion and have servants and chauffeurs. However, instead of playing the dutiful debutante who plays the violin and still has a nanny at age seventeen, Sam would rather watch ice hockey on TV and play second base on her summer softball team. Having to hide her relationship with her girlfriend, Lisa, from her parents is becoming an agonizing struggle. Not only are her friends pressuring her to come out to her parents, but they are also trying to convince her to attend a very public gay pride festival at the local college.

At least she has her nanny Helene to confide in, but for how much longer? Sam is acutely aware that the time for Helene to move on may be fast approaching. And if that isn't enough, Sam's summer softball coach gives her no end of grief after an error-filled game and isn't afraid of making an example out of her. Will Sam remain the perfect princess her parents expect? Will her beloved nanny leave her forever? Will her girlfriend get fed up about being kept hidden? Will her friends continue to pressure her about coming out? Will Coach Greer make her life miserable? All of these questions are answered in Stealing Second: Sam's Story.

ISBN: 978-1-953734-07-5 (eBook)
ISBN: 978-1-953734-19-8 (Paperback)

Out at Home
(Book Five in the Clarksonville Series)
A young adult lesbian romance

Marlee McAllister just wants to fit in. She didn't know she didn't fit in until Kate and Rita – the prettiest girls in the senior class - pointed it out. Even Marlee's grandmother declared that Marlee was too old for "this tomboy nonsense." All the other girls at school have long hair except Marlee. All the other girls wear something other than jeans, a T-shirt, and sneakers to school every day except for Marlee. All the other girls fit in except Marlee.

Marlee decides to grow out her short hair, buy femmy girly clothes, and pretend she has a boyfriend named Ronnie. Really, though? She has the most amazing girlfriend in Susie Torres. Susie is everything Marlee hoped for - sweet, sexy, kind, athletic, pretty. And best of all? She loves Marlee as much as Marlee loves her. Although their parents know about their relationship, not many other people do.

Marlee is out at home but not to anyone else. And if anyone else finds out she's into girls, Kate and Rita especially, the entire school and her grandparents will know within a day. Life as she knows it will be over.

Out at Home is the story of Marlee McAllister's life-altering struggle to fit in.

ISBN: 978-1-953734-20-4 (eBook)
ISBN: 978-1-953734-24-2 (Paperback)

Tools of the Devil
(Book Six in the Clarksonville Series)
A young adult lesbian romance

Seventeen-year-old Lisa Brown loved going to church. Oh sure, sometimes she'd rather sleep in, but she liked the calming and empowering strength of her faith. Sundays revitalized her spirit when she thanked God for the wonderful things in her life, like her loving family and amazing girlfriend, Samantha Rose. One day, she hoped to marry Sam, have a house and yard, and have babies together. One day.

But then it happened. That fateful Sunday, the guest preacher stepped behind the pulpit and spoke four words that would change Lisa's world forever. "Homosexuality is a sin," he said. Had she heard him right? She knew she had when her mother put a hand on her forearm. Every muscle in her body tensed, and she forgot to breathe. What was happening?

The church she'd been baptized in, grown up in, and wanted to get married in had, in one instant, turned against her. Still not quite believing what she'd heard, she mumbled, "Ignorance is a sin, Reverend." Never one to back down from a challenge, she scanned the congregation but didn't find a single soul who looked upset by his statement. On the contrary, many nodded in agreement. Under her breath, she muttered, "Game on, people. Game on."

ISBN: 978-1-953734-21-1 (eBook)
ISBN: 978-1-953734-25-9 (Paperback)

Going Under
(Book Seven in the Clarksonville Series)
A young adult lesbian romance

Susie Torres is a second-semester senior with devoted friends and an amazing girlfriend in Marlee McAllister. Susie's father has a job that takes him away from home on frequent business trips, but lately, his trips seem to be longer and more frequent. Tensions rise at home when Susie's mother challenges him about that. At first, Susie and her younger brother Miguel hide in her room when their parents' frequent squabbles elevate to out-and-out yelling matches. But as her parents' war escalates further, Susie finds other ways to escape the tension.

A fake ID becomes a clear and easy way to anesthetize herself with alcohol. Her crumbling home life becomes momentarily forgotten whenever she swims in a sea of peaceful drunken bliss. Unfortunately, Susie doesn't realize she is alienating everyone around her with her attempts to cope with her parents' possible divorce, including Marlee. Her best friend Sam tries to warn her that her excessive drinking is driving away all of her friends, but Sam's well-meaning advice isn't heard. Will Susie finally realize that her own actions are making her life fall apart around her? That her new love of drinking is getting in the way of everything good in her life? That her amazingly patient girlfriend isn't going to put up with much more?

ISBN: 978-1-953734-22-8 (eBook)
ISBN: 978-1-953734-26-6 (Paperback)

Stealing Hope
(Book Eight in the Clarksonville Series)
A young adult lesbian romance

Sam Payton is a high school senior with a bit of an identity crisis. Raised in a well-to-do family, she dutifully plays the role of Samantha Rose Payton, the wealthy debutante. Now, almost one full year into her life-changing relationship with Lisa Brown, Sam is hit with many life-challenging events. Her best friend, Susie Torres, struggles with alcohol addiction and a wrecked home life as her parents go through a bitter divorce, and Sam tries to help her friend keep her head above water. In another struggle, two friends cross the line between friendship and intimacy—a line that should not have been approached. Sam finds herself trying to make them see how incredibly egregious the transgressions are for all involved. And to top it all off, Sam's mother is diagnosed with a serious illness.

Through the love of her parents and her girlfriend, Sam navigates these challenges the best way she can, all while trying to fulfill everyone's varying expectations of her. Sam struggles to break free of the preconceived roles she seems bound by to figure out who she really is. It ultimately comes down to whether Sam can make everyone see that she is both a softball-playing, ice-hockey-loving lesbian named Sam as well as a classically-music-trained debutante named Samantha Rose.

ISBN: 978-1-953734-23-5 (eBook)
ISBN: 978-1-953734-27-3 (Paperback)

THE GIRLS' SPORTS SERIES (Children's Books Ages 9-12)

Bases Loaded

Sixth-grader Mackenzie Kelly's first love was soccer until her best friend talked her into playing summer softball. Now Mack is eager to be on her school's softball team and dreams of playing in the Olympics with her idol, Cat Osterman. But first, she needs to bring up her failing English grade to stay on the team. When she learns softball has been cut from the Olympics, she's determined somehow to get it back into the Olympic Games so she can fulfill her dream.

*"I just wanted to let you know I received the book and
I think it is FANTASTIC!"*
– Jessica Mendoza, *US Olympic Softball Team*

ASIN: B00094IT3RK (eBook)
ISBN 978-1-960373-35-8 (Paperback)

Side Out

Seventh-grader Dina Jacobs feels like she's landed on another planet when her family moves from Long Island, New York to Indiana. She tries out for the seventh-grade volleyball team, and her new friend, Christine, introduces her to Olympic volleyball. Now, Dina dreams of playing in the Olympics like her newfound idol, Logan Tom. Indiana doesn't seem so bad until Dina's Jewish faith crashes against her coach's win-at-all-costs attitude. Miserable, Dina is torn between staying true to her religious customs or putting them aside to play the game she loves.

ASIN: B005HM9CUU (eBook)
ISBN 978-1-934452-65-3 (Paperback)

Live, Love, Lacrosse

Addie Coleburn, fresh out of the sixth grade, is spending the summer at her grandmother's house in Syracuse with her mother and brother. Kimi Takahashi, a girl who lives up the street, invites Addie to go to the park and play lacrosse. Addie hasn't the first clue what lacrosse is and would rather sit on Grandma's front porch eating potato chips, drinking sodas, and reading books. But then again, spending the summer dealing with her younger brother isn't appealing, either, so she goes to the park with Kimi. Within a week, she's hooked on lacrosse. She's overweight and can't keep up with the faster, stronger girls. She has to find a way to lose her excess weight quickly or risk getting cut from the team.

ASIN: B09GPYMHDK (eBook)
ISBN 978-1-943837-50-2 (Paperback)

www.ingramcontent.com/pod-product-compliance
Lightning Source LLC
Chambersburg PA
CBHW051513170626
46811CB00002B/808